Gathering the Water

Gathering
the Water

ROBERT EDRIC

Doubleday

LONDON · TORONTO · SYDNEY · AUCKLAND · JOHANNESBURG

TRANSWORLD PUBLISHERS
61–63 Uxbridge Road, London W5 5SA
a division of The Random House Group Ltd

RANDOM HOUSE AUSTRALIA (PTY) LTD
20 Alfred Street, Milsons Point, Sydney,
New South Wales 2061, Australia

RANDOM HOUSE NEW ZEALAND LTD
18 Poland Road, Glenfield, Auckland 10, New Zealand

RANDOM HOUSE SOUTH AFRICA (PTY) LTD
Isle of Houghton, Corner of Boundary Road & Carse O'Gowrie,
Houghton 2198, South Africa

Published 2006 by Doubleday
a division of Transworld Publishers

A catalogue record for this book is available from the British Library.
ISBN 0385603126
9780385603126 (Jan 07)

Typeset in 11/14pt Caslon by Falcon Oast Graphic Art Ltd.

Printed in Great Britain by
Clays Ltd, St Ives plc

3 5 7 9 10 8 6 4 2

Papers used by Transworld Publishers are natural, recyclable products made from
wood grown in sustainable forests. The manufacturing processes conform
to the environmental regulations of the country of origin.

For Hilary Aikman

Part One

The appointment was announced yesterday of Mr Charles Weightman, formerly of the Hampshire Water Company, to act as overseer to the drowning of the Forge Valley. The Forge Valley Reservoir has been three years in preparation, and its dam was completed in April of this year. It is anticipated that fully another half year will elapse before the greater effects of the scheme become apparent and its benefits reaped. It is expected that Mr Weightman will lodge in the district, better able there to account for any business arising in connection with the removal of the inhabitants and the gathering of the water.

Leeds Intelligencer
Thursday, 27 October 1848

I was surprised upon my arrival here to find so many of the dwellings still inhabited. Surprised, too, and disappointed, to see so great a number of buildings where I had expected only a few, and those empty and awaiting the water. To hear the Board men speak, you might think I had been bound for a wilderness of unmapped moor crying out only for the civilizing of their scheme. To hear those men speak, you might think I had been handed the crown and sceptre of a fabulous kingdom, as yet unexplored, and over which I exercised sole and absolute dominion. I see now, looking about me, why they might have encouraged me in such a belief.

From where I stand I can see thirty smoking chimneys – signifying what? A hundred, two hundred people, where I had anticipated only a resentful and stubborn handful. The smoke from the stacks seldom rises more than a few feet before being drawn off and dispersed by the constant winds which are a chronic feature of the region.

Study the appearance of the remaining specimens, they told me. See how they are moulded by those cold winds just as an exposed tree might be twisted and stunted by them. And from what little I have so far seen of these people – their latest misfortune notwithstanding – they are undoubtedly formed in constant expectation of some hardship or other, of which, judging by the history and the stark, sour look of the place, there is a constant and never-ending supply.

It is a sooty smoke, the sign of poor or mixed fuel, fine and pale one moment, and then billowing and filled with black the next, with glowing embers rising and vanishing as they are caught in the currents of air.

An hour of daylight remained to me upon my arrival, during which I waited for the carter with my cases. He came two hours after darkness, seemingly unconcerned by the length of his return journey or by the impenetrable night through which he would make it. I asked him if he were a local man, or if he knew of anyone close by with whom he might stay, but he shook his head to both questions. It did not occur to me to offer him the use of my own ample lodgings.

He left me, and carrying no light he was quickly lost to the darkness.

I looked up, and because the moon was full and close, I saw clearly Cain and his thorns. The Fish glittered on the horizon, and the Bear sat directly over Caurus, whose presence I felt to my bones.

With regard to warmth and comfort there was little to

choose between indoors and out. I stamped and banged around the empty house as though I were a small crowd.

This writing is thirty minutes' work, and I wish only that I were more wearied by it and by my long journey and better able to sleep.

2

My first visitor came today. It has been a clear, fine day, but rather than begin my outdoor work, I have been occupied in unpacking and investigating further my new home. I cannot question why the house was chosen for me – the views from its front are extensive – but a man used to the diversions and amenities of city living or a more sociable existence might wish for a better appointed place.

You are chosen in part for your tact and adaptability, I was told, already swollen with flattery and gilded with distant authority.

My visitor came up the hillside and stopped in front of the house, where the entrance gate once stood. He had with him four rangy hounds, which settled themselves around him where he waited. I had seen him coming from a great distance because of the slope. He neither knocked nor called, and it occurred to me that he had come believing the house still to be empty. I had been looking out all morning for my first delegation, the salvo of my opening speech – Caesar-like in its tact – long since primed.

After several minutes, and because my visitor showed no sign of either leaving or approaching closer, I went out to him.

I introduced myself, and was about to say more when he interrupted me and said he knew already why I was there. The largest of his dogs bared its teeth and growled at me. He silenced it with a word. Slaver hung in strings from the creature's mouth.

'Then you have been waiting for me,' I said boldly, hoping to learn more by this directness than by other means. Here, I guessed, was a messenger, whose knowledge of me might spread like a fire.

'I have come to show you something,' he said, each word emphatically pronounced. I saw then that his own careful preparations had also been made. Much of his face was hidden by his beard, and by the grey side-whiskers which grew unchecked across his cheeks.

'Show me what?' I had been told to expect land claims and property deeds thrust in my face, disputed mining and grazing rights, rights of forage and turbage. But this man had none of those things. He took several paces back from me. 'I'm a very busy man,' I said. 'As I'm sure you can appreciate.'

'We are all busy men here,' he said. If he was insulted by my remark then he was little dissuaded by it, and he continued to savour the moment of his coming revelation.

He proceeded to take off his boots. He wore nothing beneath them and his shins and feet were as dark and scarred as his hands. He laid his boots on the wall and came closer to me, grinning broadly.

Then he shouted at me – a cry which surprised me – and pointed down at his feet with both hands. 'Look! Look!' he shouted, stepping from the grass on to the stone slabs of the path. The closest of his dogs shied away from him. At first I could see nothing, but then he raised one foot, grabbed it in both hands and pulled wide his toes. 'Raise your flood as high as you like, for I shall not drown,' he shouted.

'What in God's name are you talking about?' I said, and for the first time I felt myself threatened by his presence.

'Your flood, your water. I shall not drown. Look! Look!' He nodded to the foot he still held. 'See.' And he pulled his toes even further apart, revealing the membrane which stretched between them and joined them like the foot of a giant frog. And seeing my surprise at this – though in truth it was surprise more at the manner of the revelation than the thing itself, and as much at the animal-like stripes of clean and dirty skin as at the webbing – he lowered the one foot and raised the other to reveal the same thing there.

'What?' I said, wanting to let him know that I was not so impressed as he had hoped. 'What do you want me to say? It surely isn't such a rare occurrence.'

But he refused to be pricked into defeat. 'I shall swim,' he shouted. 'Your water shall come and I shall carry on living here, swimming from place to place just as easily as a man might now walk.' There was by then an excessive wetness on his lips.

'But everything here, all these places, will eventually be

beneath the water. How will you swim to them? The whole of the land will be changed. There will be nowhere to swim *to*.'

'I shall swim *down* to them. I shall swim on top of the water and I shall swim *beneath* it.' He lowered his foot and swung his arms as he spoke. 'My hands also,' he shouted, thrusting his hands at me, palm up, palm down.

'What of them?'

'They too were once connected in the same fashion, but were cut by a surgeon when I was a boy.'

I almost laughed at the dry note of distant regret in his voice.

'Then stay and swim,' I said to this frog-man.

'I shall.'

'And what will you live on? Fish?'

The question stopped him. 'Will there be *fish* in the new sea?'

I did not know. Somewhere in the bundles of unread reports and assessments I had brought with me there would be something said about fish.

'Of course there will be fish,' I told him.

'Then I shall live off them.' He chewed the air.

I turned and left him, remarking on the business I had yet to attend to, and he, in turn, went back to the wall and put on his boots. He went down the hillside in a zig-zag, as though uncertain of the route he wanted to take, of where he might perhaps locate the first of the rising water. And one by one, because even in those untethered lives an order existed, the dogs rose from the grass and walked behind him.

As I was about to re-enter the house I looked beyond it to the crest of the hill and saw there someone else silhouetted against the growing light. I shielded my eyes, and as I looked more closely this single watcher divided and became two, and I saw that these two were women. I saw by their movement and by the arms still held between them that one had been holding the other and that now this second figure was drawing away from the first. Thus separated, they stood motionless and looked down at me. I raised my hand to them, but received no acknowledgement. I considered climbing the short distance towards them, but some instinct – something, perhaps, connected to the way they still stood, apart and yet within reach of each other; the way the arms of one still seemed protectively half raised towards the other – kept me where I stood.

We observed each other like this for a short while, after which the taller of the two women pulled the other back to her, held her by her shoulders and then turned her away from me.

3

I have chosen the largest of the downstairs rooms for my workplace. Three heavy tables gathered in from the rest of the house will serve for my charts and plans. The fire is already laid and burning. Fires here are kept alight continuously throughout the winter, of which autumn and spring are lesser parts, and from which, seemingly, the summer is no more than a brief and unreliable reprieve.

It is a damp room, but I hope that the fire and the passage of air will keep this at bay and away from my papers. None of the Board men knew for certain how long the house had been standing empty, only that it had once belonged to a landlord here in the middle realm of the valley and that it had been quickly given up by him at their first offer of payment. I have with me the precise equations by which these sums were calculated and then pared down until the bones of double-sided greed lay exposed. I can see what a fortune it must have seemed to the landlord, what a bargain to those men of the Board.

The room has other advantages. From its two windows I have a view over the width of the valley along almost half its length. Except, that is, on days such as today, when the rising mist or falling cloud obscures everything but the upper or lower slopes.

My charts and instruments are already spread around the tables in the hope that they will deflect all enquiries and demands. The map entrusted to me showing the final extent of the water I will keep well hidden until the reality of the changes outside is all too apparent to be ignored.

There is a single picture left hanging in the house, a poor print of a martyred saint – the designation does not say which – resembling, as I imagine all martyred saints must, martyred Christ himself, and holding in his hands a cross and a bird, which, in the poor light, might – not inappropriately – easily be mistaken for a plump fish.

There is no water piped into the house, but a short distance away is a clean and reliable spring, boxed in with slabs of slate, and with a trough set into the slope beneath it in which the water settles clear.

I was told that I would be met upon my arrival, or shortly afterwards, by another of the Board's employees, a bailiff called Ellis, but the man has not yet made himself known to me.

Earlier, I spent an hour with a rusted saw levelling the uneven legs of the tables, but everywhere I lay my hand there remains imbalance.

The smoke from my resurrected fire later dislodged some soot, which fell in the afternoon and laid its fine black dust over everything I had set out.

4

It is six months since the completion of the dam, and two since the first of its sluices was closed. The plans of the structure make it appear far grander than it actually is. Elsewhere the Board might incorporate some ornamentation into its architecture – some memorial to a founder member, a nod at passing fashion – but here there is nothing, not even the small towers by which most of its other dams are anchored to their shores.

I cannot see the structure from my lodgings, but I have already walked to the scarp overlooking it. Several dwellings and a small mill were demolished to make way for it, and other buildings now stand close by: those to be drowned by it, and those to stand abandoned in its shadow.

The water, when fully collected, will rise to half the

height of the dam. The outer wall is sheer, faced with gritstone blocks, already darkening. The inner wall, that to be submerged, is raised in a gradual curve. Here, too, it is faced, but the blocks are less precisely arranged. The centre of the dam is of rubble fill and poured lime. Again unlike dams elsewhere, there is no walkway along the top of the structure, only the exposed rim left unsecured against the elements. The surface is broad enough, and the blocks set level enough for a man to lead a horse across, but there is no connecting road or path at either side, only the exposed rock of the blasted hillside.

The valley downriver runs in a series of overgrown gorges until the water reaches its mother flow. By contrast, the land above the dam is broad and open. Downriver, the dwellings and mills are of necessity tightly gathered, surrounded by woodlands and small pastures, whereas upriver the dwellings are scattered and the only cultivated land is either taken in close by them or alongside the river on its small flood plain.

You might say the world was conveniently divided here, and that the dam was its neatly drawn line.

5

'My name is Mary Latimer,' she said at the instant of our unexpected encounter. She held out her hand to me. I was becoming accustomed to such abruptness – forthrightness, they would call it – but there was something in the woman's manner and in her formality, her gentility almost, which led me to respond more cautiously.

I introduced myself.

'There is not a single person here who does not already know you,' she said. 'And, as you must be well aware, that which they do not know about you they can easily imagine.'

'And those who do not possess the imagination?'

'Oh, lies, half-truths, speculation.' She smiled at this, and though she remained reluctant to look me in the eye, I felt then as though an understanding existed between us. I knew from her voice, her choice of words and her accent, by the way she held herself, and by her reserve, that she too in some way stood apart from the place and its people.

I guessed her age to be between fifty-five and sixty. Her grey hair was held back from her forehead in a tortoiseshell comb. Strands hung by her ears, and she smoothed these back into place as she spoke. Her face, too, bore none of the more usual marks of age and hardship with which I was already familiar. Her skin was pale and little lined; her teeth even and white.

'Do you live here?' I asked her.

'I have done for the past ten months. Before that I lived here as a girl and young woman.' She looked around her as she spoke.

'And are you back here because of the dam?'

'Because everything is to be lost? Yes, in a sense. I am here to take care of my sister.' At this last word she turned from me, and I knew then that she and her sister had been my silent watchers of several days previously.

'You were on the hill,' I said.

'You raised your hand to us. You must consider us unforgiveably rude.' She went on before I could answer her. 'My sister is not well. We heard the raised voice of your visitor. She was alarmed by his dogs. Tell me, will the water come this far up the valley?' There was no pause in her speech as the subject was changed and I was diverted from talk of her sister.

'It can rise no higher than the height of the dam,' I said, and regretted the glib remark immediately.

'I meant will there be changes this far upriver? I know the hills will not be drowned.' She continued to look

around us. She showed neither anger nor remorse for all
that was to be lost.

'Where were you before returning?' I said.

'I've lived in many places. Some close by.'

'But this is where your sister lives?'

'This is where our parents lived. Lived and died. She
and I were born here.'

'And do you still feel some affection for the place?'

'Very little. Surely, you must have heard from others
about us. Surely, someone has said something. If not of me,
then of her.' She looked hard at me to determine whether
my answer was an honest one.

'Your name may be somewhere in my ledgers,' I said.

'My sister was committed to an asylum, in Colne,
twenty-seven years ago. We still lived here then, with our
parents. And last year she was released into my care and
she would live nowhere else.'

'Because this was all she knew?'

'No. But she would go nowhere else.'

'And is she . . . I mean . . .'

'Is she well? She is an old woman, two years my junior.'

'I'm sorry,' I said, and again I regretted the remark.

'No, I am the one who should apologize. I thought you
knew. We are a constant topic of conversation, she and I.
We keep ourselves apart, you see. Or, rather, *I* keep us
apart. I imagined you knew about her and were avoiding
saying anything.'

'I know what it's like to be talked about and to be kept
apart,' I said.

'I imagine you do. But you possess a power that neither
she nor I possess.'

I acknowledged the truth of this.

'And now we must leave again,' she said.

She told me the name of their home and where it stood, but it meant nothing to me. I told her I would visit her, expecting her to make some excuse to keep me away, but instead she said she would be pleased to see me.

I sensed that she was about to leave.

'Have arrangements been made?' I said.

'Arrangements?'

'By the Board. For you and your sister. A new home.'

'I'm afraid neither she nor I meet your Board's exacting requirements. No, I am making all my own arrangements.' She gave a cold, hard emphasis to the word.

Before I could ask her any more, she again held out her hand, turned and left me.

I saw by the strides she took and by her pace over the uneven ground that, despite her age, and despite the fact that she was clearly accustomed to surroundings more comfortable, varied and stimulating, she was in no way unequal to this place and its demands.

6

Some of my charts contain very little detail of the land they cover. Some leave vast spaces blank, noting only prominent streams and landmarks, of which there are few. Not even a sketched tree or sheep or rabbit in place of those grinning fish spouting on the surface of unfathomed oceans. A man who was lost here would not find himself on these charts.

My initial response to this lack of information was one of enthusiasm: here was a place I might construct to my own design in its emptiness; a place I might map into existence as though it truly were my own small domain. But in harbouring such despotic intentions I had reckoned without the place itself.

Carrying my heavy instruments to these high places has proved an impossibility, and although recordings might be

taken and heights and distances calculated in my notebooks, any attempt to unroll a sheet of mapping paper and
plot these with any degree of accuracy in the field is
impossible on all but the stillest of days, and the present
season is not renowned for those.

There is no distinct line of divide marking this valley
from the one to the north, only a pale track winding across
the peat top. In the prospectus to investors there is
mention of vividly yellow gorse blazing here and there like
fires in the wilderness. These are no longer in flower, but
might be eagerly imagined amid such dullness.

The head of the valley is a confused place. Where
elsewhere a river might rise out of the ground flowing from
a spring, here the water draining from the peat forms itself
into countless shifting channels, most no broader than my
arm. In some places these have created valleys in
miniature; elsewhere a flow forms in the impression of my
heel, collects and then runs off.

Yesterday I walked up the valley as far as the lead mines
and their spoil heaps. I was surprised by the size of the
buildings, by the substance of their construction in so in-
accessible a place, and by the great extent of their spilled
waste, hillocks piled one upon the other running from the
mines to the valley bottom, and looking from a distance
like giant eggs laid neatly out across the slope.

7

This is my first stay in the north of any length and already I have started gathering the details by which the true spirit of the place might be best understood, and which, to my naturalist's mind at least, are worthy of record.

Those peat tops, for instance, are everywhere called 'hags'; the viper or adder is a 'hagworm'; the kestrel is a 'windhover'; the snail a 'wallfish'; and the rowan tree is still without reservation referred to as 'witchwood'.

Long before my arrival, but upon learning of my appointment, I was warned by my acquaintances – now mostly lost – that the language, manners and customs of the place would be in great measure unintelligible, and, where intelligible, then repulsive to me. I feigned concurrence with this advice, and then humour at every joke it spawned.

There are twenty names for the various rains which fall, and which often vary within a single shower. A storm of less than a day's duration is a 'small' storm, and the thrush is without fail called 'stormcock' because of its perverse habit of turning into every wind and whistling undisturbed by it.

8

I went into that part of the lower valley where the dwellings are greater in number. Most are on the same side of the river, the opposite bank immediately above and below the dam being steeper and wooded. I went to observe the flow of the river below the dam now that its sluices are in operation and the movement of the water regulated. I have no power over the working of the dam. The bailiff alone – should he ever reveal himself to me – possesses that in conjunction with the distant controllers and planners.

The flow was greatly reduced, revealing the gravel and boulders of the river-bed. Stepping stones rose in short pillars like the remains of a lost colonnade. I noted down everything I saw. The few people I encountered either ignored me or departed having exchanged the obligatory cold pleasantries.

Another purpose of my visit there was to establish some means of communication with the outer world. I shall let the phrase stand; it is how I feel. The mail coach passed on the main road eight miles to the south, but I was as yet unsure how to make my connection with it. The Board men had seemed little concerned regarding this difficulty.

Leaving the river, I climbed the bank and returned among the houses, and there I again encountered Mary Latimer. She emerged from a walled alley, a package of letters in her hand, which she inspected as she walked. I called to her and she stopped. I approached her and apologized for having interrupted her. She seemed relieved that it was I who had called and not someone else. A group of women stood a short distance from us, each of them having turned at my call.

'Are you working?' she said. She returned the gaze of the women, but this did little to dissuade them from watching us.

I indicated her letters and told her why I was there. 'You appear to have a great many correspondents,' I said.

'A week's gleanings.' It was still an impressive number. She told me the name of the man who brought the mail from the coach. She pointed to his home at the far end of the walled lane. Pieces of furniture stood around the house.

'Will he too soon be gone?'

'I imagine so.'

'And what then?'

'Then another door will be heard slamming loudly shut behind us. You must surely be familiar with the sound by now.'

'They tend to slam shut ahead of me,' I said, thus leavening our conversation. I made a note of the man's name. 'Will he insist on me coming to collect my mails?' I asked, hoping to suggest to her that it would be arriving sufficiently frequently for this to be an inconvenience to me.

She shrugged. 'I am only forced to come myself because I refuse to pay more than I was originally charged.'

'Is your home far?'

She indicated the steep hillside behind us, but without turning. 'A mile, perhaps a little further.'

'Are you alone?'

'Is my sister with me, you mean.'

'It wasn't my intention to intrude.'

'Yes, I came down alone. There are still a few here brave enough to visit us and sit with her on the rare occasions I am obliged to leave her. There are still those who remember us as girls, who knew our parents.'

Having stood for a minute, she seemed suddenly impatient to leave me. Perhaps the talk of her sister had reminded her of some ever-present responsibility. And yet even as I discerned this, I sensed too that she was savouring her brief freedom.

'I will not turn her into more of a spectacle than she has already become,' she said, her eyes flicking towards the watching women.

'Would it disappoint you to learn that they were watching me walk up and down the dead river long before you appeared?'

She smiled at this. 'Then what a bonus for them. The two of us together. The twin serpents of madness and destruction entwined, and in full view of honest, decent, hard-working, God-fearing folk such as themselves.'

She resumed walking and I walked alongside her.

We approached the women, but rather than turning away from us or dispersing as I had expected, they held their ground, their arms folded defiantly in front of them. It was a feature of these women, when talking in a group, to fall silent on a single beat at the appearance of anyone unwanted or unknown to them, their concerted silence and cold stares intimidating the newcomers into turning away from them and warning those who had perhaps intended to join them not to attempt to do so.

In this respect they were different from their men, who would continue to talk loudly, even if the intruder were the subject of their discussion, as I had learned to my cost on several occasions.

It was not tact or shame which created these silences in the women, merely a form of expediency which, once acknowledged by the newcomer, allowed them to continue uninterrupted.

Mary Latimer said 'Good morning' to them and they murmured their reply.

We continued beyond them to the edge of the dwellings, where she stopped and said that this was where we parted.

'I thought I might walk to your home with you,' I said. I had made no plans for the remainder of the day.

She looked directly at me. 'Oh?'

'Unless you would prefer to return alone.'

'You know exactly what I am thinking, Mr Weightman.'

It was the first time anyone there had called me by my name, and hearing it caught me momentarily off balance.

'You see how protective I am of her, even with people who know her.'

'And I am a complete stranger to you.'

'Surely you must entertain some apprehension about meeting a madwoman?'

My own mother, upon losing her second child, had been sent away to a sanatorium recommended by a colleague of my father. She had stayed there for four months before returning to us. I was seven years old at the time and the months had seemed like years to my young mind.

'I would not wish to inconvenience her,' I said.

'You mean unsettle. You may say it.'

I said nothing.

'There are some here who would find it easier to lose their sight than their opinion on the subject.'

'By which you mean prejudice,' I said. 'You would misjudge me to include me among them.'

She acceded to this. 'I know that.' She searched through the letters she carried and pulled one out. 'This is a communication from the director of the new asylum to which I shall shortly take her.'

'But I thought . . .'

'Thought what, Mr Weightman? That she and I might find some new, secure and secluded place in which to live out the remainder of our lives together?'

'Is it what you want – the asylum?'

'It was my decision to make enquiries about the place. Perhaps one day in every five she has some slight and fleeting understanding of what is happening around her, but for the remainder of the time she wanders a strange land among strangers. At least there they will be able to care for her.'

I could see that it pained her to tell me these things, and only later did it occur to me that I might have been the only one in the valley to whom she had spoken of the place.

'It distresses you to talk of it,' I said.

'The situation distresses me. Speaking of it – speaking of it to someone who has little or no connection to it – is of no consequence whatsoever to me.'

She continued walking and made no further objection when I walked alongside her.

'Except, of course,' I said after several minutes had passed silently between us, 'that I am here to drown your home, flood your childhood haunts and drive you both out into an uncaring world.'

'Ah, I'd forgotten. Yes, except for that.' She put her hand on my shoulder, as though to console me for my burden. 'There is another communication you might be interested to see,' she said. She took a second envelope from the package. I recognized it immediately as coming from the Board, and my envy at her mails was instantly doubled. 'You yourself are no doubt all too familiar with such platitudinous irrelevancies,' she said.

I shrugged to suggest my unhappy concurrence, and before either of us could speak again she tore the unopened envelope and unread letter into scraps and threw them up into the air.

'You could retrieve all the pieces on your way back down,' she said, fully aware of my discomfort at what she had done. 'Take them home with you and reassemble them like a puzzle.' She paused and looked at the scattered white all around her, tatters of which still floated in the air. 'As big a puzzle, in fact, as why you were ever sent here in the first place.'

I felt stung by the remark. 'Oh? And more or less

puzzling than the fact that you removed your sister from her previous asylum?'

If I expected the remark to silence or provoke her, then I was disappointed.

'No mystery there, Mr Weightman. Money. There is nothing left. Little enough to sustain us as we are. The dregs of a few long-depleted investments. Perhaps I should have gathered together what little remained and handed it over to your masters to invest in their lake. Would the irony of such a gesture be lost on them, do you think?'

'Undoubtedly.' It was an answer where none was called for.

We had come most of the way up the slope. She stopped and pointed out to me a house which had until then been hidden by the curve of the land. 'Our home,' she said.

'And you are going to insist again that I can come no further with you.'

'And you are going to look more closely and see my sister waiting for me at the gate.'

I looked and saw the distant woman. She stood by the wall of the small enclosure which surrounded the house.

'And I, of course, having already come so far against your wishes, am in no position to refuse you,' I said.

'Of course.'

I looked again, and this time saw the outline of a second woman standing in the doorway behind the first.

'You would be wise not to tell the mail carrier that you come on my recommendation,' she said, both drawing me back to her and returning me to my original errand.

I held up my hands to her in defeat.

'And it was a great pleasure to have had your company and conversation,' she said.

'Yours, too.'

'Offer him half of what he asks. The more you receive, the lower his price should be.'

'Ah,' I said.

She laughed aloud at this, understanding perfectly my predicament. 'Now I regret even more having torn up my own letter.'

She walked away from me, waving vigorously as she went. I watched for some response from the woman by the gate, but there was none.

9
_____

The occasion of my interview was my first visit to Halifax, and I was surprised to find the town so obviously prosperous. None of my interviewers lived in the town itself – they all had their 'places' in the improved country surrounding it – but this was where they made their fortunes and where all their business was conducted.

It occurred to me even at our first meeting that here were men who had already made their decision concerning my appointment, and that I was there with them, in the Commercial Hotel, merely for them to confirm the strengths and weaknesses of my abilities and character, upon which they were already decided.

I met with various of the men on each of the three days I stayed in the town, but I can say with absolute conviction that anything of any real value which needed to be imparted to me might have been usefully said in under an hour. Some – particularly the more senior members of the Board – were there merely so that I might acknowledge their presence. I flattered myself then that they, in some unspoken reciprocal arrangement, might take an interest in my work, even if only because of the connection between it and their own ever-growing fortunes.

Some of my questions – I had prepared many – set several of my interviewers ill at ease, and some of what I asked them they treated as a private joke.

There was a further great plan to rebuild the sewers of the town, and then those of the towns and cities close by, and it was suggested that the reservoir, and others like it, might one day become a vital part of these schemes, thereby becoming greatly increased in value.

One man, the Director of Procurement, told the story of a piece of land he had bought several years previously upon hearing that a new railway branch line was to be built. He calculated the likely route of the line in advance of even the railway engineers and then sought out all the possible land for sale along it. Other speculators had the same idea, he said, and they all paid high prices for the narrow corridors of land upon which the railway, in their estimation, would be forced to run. But this man did not want that. He professed himself an expert in the construction of tunnels and predicted great advances in the field. To that end he bought a spur of high land over which the railway would be unable to climb, and which was too extensive to be dug through. He bought this land for a fraction of what the others had paid, and then he waited. And when the railway finally did come – and with it his predicted advances in tunnel-building – he sold the right of passage at a great profit. And then he sold the excavated rock for use elsewhere. And afterwards, when the railway was built and running, he reacquired the land above the tunnel for his own use.

He counted off these gains on his fingers as he spoke. It was an easy enough lesson for me to learn and to remember.

10

'John Wesley himself, the preacher John Wesley, he sermoned at that chapel.'

Of course he did. And at every other fallen-down hen-coop and walled midden in this valley and the dozen valleys on either side of it.

'John Wesley the preacher?' I said, my tone even.

The man nodded vigorously. I guessed him to be sixty-five or seventy, though he may have been younger by ten years. He leaned on the chapel wall. I knew something of Wesley, of his work and conversions in the district, and I knew that the old man himself could never have met him except possibly as a very small child.

'You attended here?' I said.

'John Wesley himself,' he said. 'Come all the way down

from Hawes on horseback through a storm.'

And if it hadn't been Wesley then history would have fractured again and it would have been George Fox or Father Grimshaw, building chapels with their bare hands and spending a month on the conversion of a single soul.

I had tried the chapel door and found it locked. Arrangements were already under way to exhume and remove the few dozen bodies the small burial ground still held. The place had never been licensed for baptisms or marriages.

Wesleyans, Methodists, Independent Methodists, Quaker Methodists, Methodist Unitarians, Primitives, New Connectioners. Even Magic Methodists. It would not surprise me to have to add the odd tribe of Jumpers or Tenters to the list.

'Man is a poor, blind, fallen, wretched, miserable, help-less sinner without grace,' he said. And if this applied to him, too, then he seemed proud to be in possession of any or all of those attributes. Or perhaps we had all already sinned away our Day of Grace without being in the slightest degree aware of it.

'Do you have relatives buried here?' I asked him.

The question surprised him and he considered it without answering me. 'All truth is in the Bible,' he said. 'I never knew a man, woman or child to find truth outside of it.'

Most of the graves were undistinguished, many unmarked by even the simplest stone. The few small memorials still standing bore only the necessary details of names and dates and those left behind to mourn, and most of these had been long since tilted and planed by the wind.

'You know what they say,' he said.

It did not matter whether or not I knew what *they* said.

He went on: 'Wesleyanism is the religion for the poor.'
And Primitive Wesleyanism the religion *of* the poor.

'And?' I prompted him.

'And Primitive Wesleyanism the religion *of* the poor.'
This revelation pleased him and he waited for my response
to his cleverness, which is certainly what he considered
it to be.

A solitary thorn grew alongside the building; no mourn-
ing yew here.

'There was never an Israelite in this valley,' he said,
causing me to wonder if our 'conversation' had not taken
some other course without my realizing it.

'And now never shall be,' I said.

'That's right.'

'So you see another benefit of the water.'

My irony was lost on him and he turned away from me to
look out over the valley bottom. I had heard it said in
Halifax that one unexpected benefit of the flooding was
that it would eradicate for ever poverty in the valley.

'My father said that the number of conversions at any
meeting or revival could be predicted here by counting the
number of fish gathered in that pool.' He pointed to where
the pool no longer stood, already lost beneath the flooded
skim of meadow. But he still saw it. 'Five fishes, five men
converted.'

After that we stood in silence for several minutes.

Then he said, 'And when will the dead arise?'

'On Judgement Day, surely.'

'I mean our dead.' He indicated the burial ground.

'The diggers are contracted before the end of the year.'
It was as much as I knew. It was part of my work to visit
each of the families concerned. Thus far I had found only

six among the living who still cared for the treatment of the dead. It would have been considerably easier and cheaper merely to remove the remaining headstones and to leave the graves undisturbed. There was a new burial ground, seven miles distant, still more field than cemetery, to which all the dead of the valley were to be removed. Any compensation for whatever loss this removal entailed was absorbed in the cost of digging, carting and reburial.

'Where are your own family buried?' he said.

'My parents in Hampshire.'

He shook his head, puzzled; the place did not exist.

And Helen, dead at twenty-three, at her family plot in Shrewsbury.

'You have no wife?'

'My mother died when I was a child.'

'No wife or childer of your own? You're a grown man. Were you never married? No man here, unless he is mad or cast out, is ever unwed by the time he reaches twenty-five. And even if he *is* mad or cast out he might still hope to be wed by thirty.'

Dead almost a year now, three years to the day of our meeting. My fiancée. And I wish with all my heart that it were otherwise.

'They won't come out easy,' he said.

'Who?'

'Our dead. This land is chopped out, not dug. It goes back down like iron. No plough was ever used here.'

I pitied him the lack of a skull to hold and a ham-bone to shake in my face.

11

Soon after entering this profession I was told the story of the Chinese city of Hangzhou by one of my teachers. This fabulously wealthy city was at its most magnificent during the tenth century and contained a great palace. It was a city surrounded by extensive lakes, the water of which was controlled and exploited by massive and complicated waterworks.

Sometime during the tenth century there was excessive rainfall, and flooding took place in the mountains to the west of the city. The level of the Great West Lake rose alarmingly and went on rising. Eventually a tidal wave rose at a great distance and swept towards Hangzhou, ever growing as it came, and driven by strong winds until it rose to twice the height of the city walls.

The governor at that time was a man called Qian Liu. Messengers came to him hourly with reports of this approaching wave. Thousands fled their homes towards the east. Qian Liu was petitioned to take action to save the city and the palace. He climbed a high tower and saw for himself the great and unstoppable wave, by then grown even higher. Qian Liu considered through the whole of a sleepless night how best to save the city, and the following morning, as the wall of water completed its journey towards Hangzhou, he sent out four thousand of his finest archers to line the shore of the lake, to form into double ranks there, to draw back their bows and then to fire their arrows into the wave the instant before it broke over them, and in this way destroy it.

Following our laughter, one of my fellow students asked if the plan had proved successful. Our teacher told us that no one had survived to say whether it had worked or not. There was more laughter. Then our teacher asked which of us, being in possession of four thousand archers and nothing more, and seeing what Qian Liu saw, would have done anything differently.

12

There is a place here, an abandoned barn called Low Syke, which is to be the first of the buildings lost to the reservoir. It stands in the valley bottom close upriver to the dam, and there is now a daily increase in the water filling the braided channels around it. This has not yet risen above the unfaced foundations of the dam, nor to the painted marker which will measure a depth against the dam of six feet. A pity this was not raised higher than the height of a man. Even here there must be those who attain that height.

Low Syke was once a farm, then latterly a barn for winter provender. The water has already mounted its worn step and spilled inside, most of it to soak instantly through the earthen floor, but still inside.

A crowd has gathered to witness this first identifiable

loss. Futile to point out to them that the structure was already derelict, its roof flags sagging and ready to fall with another winter, or that, being so low in the valley, it had already been inundated in a succession of past floods.

I considered it no less than my duty to mark the occasion with my presence. And, needless to say, there were those among the onlookers who resented me being there; but those too, I was gratified to find, who were beginning to show some interest in my work, and who disguised poorly their enthusiasm for their own departures. The people here seemed to me like the poor soil of the place, laid down begrudgingly generation after generation, but sustaining little, of little value, and easily lost between the rock below and the wind above.

Children paddled in the few inches of water which rose into the enclosures of Low Syke. They threw stones for the simple pleasure of causing a splash. Some of the older ones stood ready with sticks for the rats they were certain would soon emerge from the doomed building, but which, like their shipboard cousins, had gone long in advance of the water. A solitary rabbit ran awkwardly along the flooded bank of the far shore, too distant for their stones.

A shout went up to indicate when the lap of water into the empty building came level with the water outside. There cannot have been more than two inches over the whole of the barn's floor.

I went to the water's edge, and in an effort to stamp my authority upon the occasion I took out my notebook and wrote in it. Simple enough details, but ones which settled a silence around me. Another man might have listed all the other buildings to be lost and then drawn a line through the names as they went. Was a place lost when it was no longer accessible because of the build-up of water around it, when it was first breached by that water, or when the uppermost coping of its roof was finally covered? Those standing close to me looked over my shoulder at what I wrote. I noted that it was no longer raining, but that the rain from two days previously still flowed in the tan-coloured channels. I noted that in addition to the abandoned barn, the once-cultivated land of its small enclosures was also flooded.

I surreptitiously counted the number of people present and made a note of that too. It will be interesting to see how these spectators increase or decline as the process continues and they are made ever more forcibly to understand the irrevocable nature of what has been set in motion here.

I closed my notebook, fastened its thin binding and returned it to my pocket. Another man might have thought a short speech appropriate, might even have said that we were witness to History.

I returned to my lodgings following the line of the river instead of the rising track, leaving myself a steep final climb to my door. I met a man who had been present at the gathering and I learned from him that there had been other strangers there besides myself. I asked him who these men were, but he said he did not know, guessing them to have come from a neighbouring valley or one of the downriver villages. Had they expected some kind of celebration, I asked him. Again, he did not know. The world was full of men content to witness the loss and suffering of others, he said. The slope exhausted me and I stumbled frequently in the wet grass.

13

My interview and appointment, my leaving the south, my coming north: all this was to be my new start. Upon losing Helen I entered the dark, uncharted territory of grief and longing; I had no understanding then, no vague awareness, even, of the true dimensions of loss and how it might be measured, let alone how it might be contained and endured.

Starting anew, I began to discern the light and the landmarks of the possible future. There was a time in between, of course – a period of confusion in which life went on and I acted out my part within it – but it was never starting anew, never a rebirth, merely a succession of lesser endings, during which I severed my ties one after another – my family, my work, my connection to Helen's family, to her sister, to my colleagues, and finally, upon reaching the shapeless centre of that darkness, my hopes and expectations of the future.

How shocked and surprised they would all profess to be – all those others – to see this written here; how indignant or solicitous they would become.

I see now, of course, that I placed too great an emphasis on this new beginning, and that those lesser endings continue to reverberate, that I feel their chills and tremors even now. And only now, here, detached from those old foundations, am I able to understand the true nature of those losses, and the shape, too, of the mould in which I sought to form myself anew. I had hoped to be burnished by my suffering, but I was all too often doused in self-indulgence, allowing new flaws and lines of fracture to be easily established.

But I knew none of this at the time of my interview and appointment, and my hope then, for once, was as alive as a kite in a windy sky.

14

'A poet once wrote of this place that there was a vein of
hard and shining madness bred into it like a vein of
glittering quartz laid down in its otherwise unremarkable
rock.'

Mary Latimer looked slowly around us, as though the
truth of the remark might somehow be revealed to her in
what she saw.

'A poet who never spent a winter here, presumably,' I
said.

'Undoubtedly. Except what wholly sane man or woman
would want to do that? He suggested that the vein of
insanity was essential to existence here, to endurance and
survival.'

I heard in her tone how long she had been away from the

place. If there was a longing for it, then it was buried deep and unsought.

We were again alone. She had come to the house and accompanied me on my short journey to the watershed. Her first remark to me was that she was unable to stay long, that again she had left her sister in the care of someone. She asked after my mails and I told her that the theory and practice of their delivery had not, as yet, been consummated. She referred to my house as a 'misanthropist's heaven', suggesting some distant familiarity with the place. I assured her that I was no such man.

'All my own expectations would have been crushed had I stayed,' she said. 'Even now, thirty-five years on, everything here seems all too easily reduced to the equation balancing struggle and achievement against failure and loss.'

'Did you and your sister leave together?'

'We did. And lived together for a while. Until her illness parted us.'

'I searched my documents for mention of your home,' I said. It had been my intention to encourage her to tell me more, but I knew even as I spoke how committed to failure I was.

'Oh?'

'There was talk of it remaining intact, for use by the bailiff, or as a store.'

'I know.'

'They offered to buy it,' I said.

'For a fraction of its worth.'

'The report said it had been left standing empty for a considerable time.'

'I'm sure it did.'

'Why do you object to the plan?'

'I'm not sure that I do. Perhaps I only object to the principle.'

'But, surely, the money would have helped with your sister.'

'And did your report also mention how much we were offered for the house, regardless of it being used or not?'

'No, but perhaps I could make some recommendation,' I said, instantly betrayed by my lack of conviction.

'And make more trouble for yourself? Please, not on our behalf.' She looked at the watch she carried. 'He said that God had been here, had reached out to bless the place and had then withdrawn his hand at the last moment.'

'The poet?'

'I wonder if he didn't merely float over us all on a glorious summer's day in a balloon, drinking Madeira and feasting on exotic fruits.'

'We have a lot in common, he and I,' I said.

'Possibly. But he was up in the air, passing us by, and you, unfortunately, Mr Weightman, are as earthbound as the rest of us, planted here as solidly as your dam and waiting only for the water to rise up your legs and cover you.'

I laughed at this. 'Please,' I said, 'call me Charles.'

'I cannot,' she said immediately. 'It was my late husband's name.'

'And did—'

'He died two years ago.'

And with him went all the comforts and certainties of your life.

'I understand,' I said.

She considered me for a moment, and then said, 'You came expecting to find the place deserted. You cannot deny it. You came expecting to find us all gone. Otherwise they would have sent another man, someone more suited to doing what you now find yourself forced to do.'

I acknowledged the rightness of her guess and the compliment it contained.

She stood in a seeming reverie for a moment before leaving me, all sound of her passage through the heather drowned out by the soughing of the wind.

15 _____

The purpose of the early incursions by the wreckers was to demolish those dwellings that would, like Low Syke, be lost the soonest to the rising water, and to take down any prominent features of the buildings expected to succumb soon afterwards. To this end they attacked all the chimney stacks and the ventilation columns where they rose from the ground over which the water would come to rest.

The wrecking crews came with their own maps and lists of empty buildings, but mistakes were still made. Chimneys were lopped on houses still inhabited, and roofs destroyed by the toppled stacks.

On at least one occasion the wreckers were confronted and held off, and some were discovered to be local men put out of work elsewhere.

Later, once the dam was completed, the tactics of the Board changed. As individual dwellings were vacated, so the wreckers were set on them in the night. Walls were razed to the ground. All good stone and slate was taken away. Fires were made of floors and rafters, more to prevent the timbers being salvaged than to destroy them. Nearby dwellers stayed away, listening from behind locked doors to the sounds of destruction. In this way, over several months, the main part of the work was done and the people here grew accustomed to living among ruins.

All this had happened through the previous winter, when the nights were long and the days themselves dark.

Throughout the past spring and summer, however, the wreckers had come more openly. They were no longer local men. They were brought by the railway and then carried on carts, delivered and collected. They considered themselves superior men. They took pride in their brutality. Occasionally a small crowd might gather to watch them work and these men would play to their audience. One of the overseers, apparently, upon finding himself and his crew observed, had turned to the crowd and called out to them that they should consider themselves fortunate not to have possessed a church with a steeple or tower. Otherwise, he shouted gleefully, this would have been the first of his targets. The open chapel belfry rose scarcely four feet above its low roof.

I am reassured – insofar as I am reassured of anything connected to the Board – that the chapel, despite the imminent loss of its burial ground, will not be demolished, but will be left to the water.

It is the natural condition of every stone-built structure in this place to fall into ruin, and in most instances there is little to distinguish between the piles of overgrown rubble and the slopes of scree and drifted talus that occur here naturally. Wood, too, is quickly bleached to the colour of a cut stump and loses all trace of its man-made shape in the course of a year exposed to the elements.

In considering all this, I cannot ignore the obvious comparison between the wreckers and myself. These other men are skirmishers, come seemingly out of nowhere, destructive and quickly withdrawn; and, allowing the comparison, I find myself little more than a camp follower, a scavenger, benefiting from this brutality, and trudging with my account book through the aftermath, the mess and loss and suffering of battle.

Earlier today, and not for the first time, I heard myself called 'flooder'. The name and all it implies makes me smile.

16

I crossed to the far side of the middle valley and turned downriver, coming eventually to the tributary I sought. A decade ago a flood had risen in this lesser valley and had flowed disastrously into the main watercourse, killing seven men and over a hundred penned sheep. A swathe of high pasture was cut to bedrock and lost for ever. One explanation for this sudden deluge was that a great blister of moss and peat had risen following several days of heavy rainfall, that the land itself, having absorbed as much of this water as it could contain, had then turned to liquid, risen in a black dome, burst and spilled itself out along the narrow tributary with the force of a torrent and giving no warning of its rush into the main valley below. Four of the seven bodies were soon recovered, but the others were never found, not even later when the waters receded and a fuller search was made.

It occurred to me as I climbed the far side that the effects of the recent saturating rainfall might one day be felt again, and I sought out the location of the blister. The grass beneath my feet sprang water where I walked.

I eventually located a shallow crater, forty feet in diameter, and although partially regrown, this was clearly the site of the phenomenon. A broad scar of exposed rock stretched from the crater down to the stream, and the stream itself was deeper and wider beneath the mark. Inside the crater lay an almost perfectly circular pool. It was beyond me to understand how any of the drainage engineers might accurately predict the likelihood of any such recurrence, but I felt reassured by the fact that the reservoir would be sufficient in size and depth to absorb and to act as a brake on any further rapid flooding originating in the hills above it.

It was as I left this side valley that I saw a figure beneath me. A man was coming uphill with his head down, concentrating on the effort of walking. I descended and called out to him. He stopped at my cry and looked up. I saw that he was laden with satchels, that he carried a small spade, and that a chart case similar to my own hung at his side. My first thought was that here at last was the water bailiff come to introduce himself.

But instead of approaching closer, the man waited where he stood for me to come to him. In those places where the sun shone most intensely against the slope, a thin vapour rose from the grass.

'You've visited the site of the flood,' he said, and put out his hand. 'Are you the overseer?'

'And you?' I said. It only then occurred to me that he might have had some other connection to the Board.

'On a quest for Venutius. Thirty years thus far, and barely a thing found.'

'Venutius?'

'Warrior chief of the Brigantes. He broke with the ruler, Queen Cartimandua, in disgust at her passive capitulation to the Romans.' He spoke as though he had been called upon to explain himself a hundred times before.

'And you search for him here?' I looked at the emptiness all around us; it seemed no place for the romance of history.

'It was to these parts that he fled, better able to resist. He raided to the east of here for over twenty years.'

'What became of him?'

'What you would expect.'

'He disappeared into legend,' I said.

'Unhappily, no. The Romans hunted him down, killed him, killed or enslaved his family, his children and followers, and then destroyed all trace of him. And that, as I am constantly reminded, is what makes my own task so difficult.'

'Have you found nothing?'

'A few clues. Some of his followers were set to work in the first lead mines here. I daresay their descendants might still be found, though I doubt many survived for long or had the inclination to breed families of their own.' He too looked around us. 'It seems an unnatural pursuit at the best of times in these parts.'

'Is there any one thing for which you are searching?'

'A shrine. Built by the Romans to Silvanus.'

'The god of wild places,' I said. I had heard of others during my work elsewhere.

'And believed to be somewhere along the higher reaches of this valley side, or the valley adjacent.'

'And you still search for it after thirty years?'

My discouraging tone did nothing to dissuade him. 'I do,' he said. 'And if I am running around in circles, then I must start to run even faster.'

'Oh?'

'Your scheme.'

'You think the water will cover it?'

'Possibly, possibly not.' Then he asked me which direction I was walking and offered to accompany me part of the way.

'You could return to search above the level of the water,' I suggested.

'My task at present is all but impossible,' he said. 'Imagine impossibility doubled.'

I drew for him with my hand where I thought the water might come.

'I have visited the supposed grave of Agamemnon,' he said. 'He is laid beneath Mediterranean limestone, and a softer rock you never saw. The whole tomb has been hollowed out and used by bees. A grave filled with honey.'

'It seems a different thing entirely, history there and history here,' I said.

'Then you are not familiar with the *Historia Britonum*? There is a cave in the rock beneath a castle not twenty miles away in which Arthur and his knights are said to be sleeping.' He turned to look in the direction of the distant, invisible place.

'By which you mean dead and buried.'

'Legend insists they are merely sleeping, awaiting the call to awake and come to the nation's rescue.'

ROBERT EDRIC

'Rescue from what?'

'From invaders, I daresay. From men come to seize the land.'

'Then I shall seize and pillage and destroy as quietly as I know how,' I said.

He then diverted a short distance from our course and beckoned me to follow him. 'The larder of a shrike,' he said, indicating a thorn bush, the points of which were filled with the impaled bodies of insects and worms and several small frogs. He studied these and searched around us for the butcher, but the bird was not to be seen.

He explained to me that it was his belief that once, countless years ago, years beyond any biblical span or explanation, the whole of these uplands and their valleys had lain buried beneath a deep sea of ice. Ice as solid as rock, and as deep as the ice which now covered the Poles. He saw that I was not convinced by this, but went on with his description. It was his opinion that every feature of the valley could be traced back to the weight and motion of this ice, and especially its melting and draining away. Even the smallest feature, he said, might be accounted for by this cap of ice and the cataclysm of its departure.

He made the present upheaval seem as nothing by comparison with this distant event. I asked him if there had been people living here at the time of all this ice, and he told me that he believed there had been, and that it had once been his ambition to locate their remains.

I asked him to tell me more, but he became suddenly evasive on the subject, considering, perhaps, that my disbelief might turn to ridicule behind his back.

We parted where my path home crossed the river.

In later considering my conversation with the man, it

63

occurs to me that I might be said to be suffering from an opposing affliction to those sailors who, spending long periods on the open oceans, begin to imagine they can see green fields, woodland and rolling hills where, in truth, there is only the limitless sea. This affliction is called 'calenture'. But whereas they look out over the expanse of water and see those fields and woods and hills, I look out over those same features and see only the expanse of coming water. I can extend the fanciful comparison no further. Do the mariners fully recover their sanity upon reaching home, I wonder, or is it lost to them for ever in a storm of madness?

17

I went today to visit Mary Latimer and her sister. I followed a different path to the one she and I had climbed from the dam, expecting the two to intersect close to their home. Instead I was led away from where I calculated the house to be and was forced to cross a waterlogged hilltop to reach them.

Finally approaching the building, I saw immediately that it had once been more substantial than most others hereabouts, certainly better built and situated than my own, but that now it stood, if not in ruin, then in a state of considerable disrepair. It was larger than I had imagined, certainly far too large and demanding in its upkeep for the two women who now lived there. Slabs were missing from one end of its roof, and wood had been nailed over all the upstairs windows. The porch which had once surrounded the front door lay in rubble on either side of the path.

The small garden was completely overgrown, and though I saw the remains of pasture walls stretching out from the enclosure, the improved land they might once have contained was now indistinguishable from the moorland beyond.

As I approached, Mary Latimer came out to me.

'You lost your path,' she said.

I brushed at the wet stains which covered me to my knees. 'I never found it.'

'Welcome to our mansion.'

I told her I could still discern what the place had once been.

'And I sometimes wish, looking at what it has become, that you could raise your water high enough to cover it, so that it might be gone completely.'

'Is your attachment to the house strong?'

'Once it was. But, as you have already surmised, it was not then what it has become. And I am here, now, with Martha, through circumstance rather than choice.'

Martha was her sister; I had not previously known the woman's name.

'Is she well? I mean well enough to receive visitors?'

'It may seem a harsh thing to say, but how she feels is of little consequence concerning much of the life passing around her.'

'I never knew her name.'

'Martha. Sister of Lazarus. The Disappointed Woman. Shall we go in? Look over my shoulder; she will no doubt be watching us through the window. We occupy only a small part of the house: the kitchen and two of the downstairs rooms.'

I looked over her shoulder and saw the woman standing there. My apprehension regarding my introduction to her must have showed on my face.

'There's nothing to fear,' Mary Latimer said. 'There are days when she devotes far more of her energy to the passing birds than she does even to me.'

'I'm not afraid,' I said.

'Not even of offending me, perhaps, by some infelicitude or crass remark concerning her?'

'Of that, perhaps, yes.'

To reassure me further, she took me by the arm and led me into the house.

The hallway was narrow and unlit.

'Watch where you step,' she said. 'Some of the boards are rotten.' Then she called her sister's name several times, both to warn the woman of our imminent appearance, and also to reassure her, as one might repeat the name of a horse or a dog in order to calm it.

She went first into the room in which the woman awaited us. It was a room similar in many respects to my own, with its windows facing down over the slope, and with a fire in the hearth at the far end.

The woman stood at her place by the window.

'Martha, this is Mr Weightman. He is here to oversee the dam and the reservoir.' She paused, waited. 'Mr Weightman.' She stood aside so that I might present myself more fully.

The woman looked first at my face and then down to my wet legs and feet.

'He lost his path,' Mary Latimer said beside me.

The woman at the window nodded, and then she held
out her hand and came towards me. 'You should really have
come down to the dam and then up through the houses,'
she said. 'Nothing else is reliable at this time of year. Come
closer to the fire.'

I allowed her to lead me closer to the hearth. Mary
Latimer remained where she stood in the doorway.

'Please, take off your boots,' Martha said to me. She
directed me to a chair and then knelt beside me, as though
about to pull off my boots. The gesture – behaving as
though I were a close friend or acquaintance – surprised
me. I unfastened my laces.

'You're very kind,' I said.

'Oh, we know all about kindness,' she said, sharing a
glance with her sister and making it clear to me that it was
*un*kindness to which she referred.

A photographic portrait of their parents looked down at
us from the mantel, still a benign presence in the house.
Mary Latimer saw me looking and nodded to confirm my
guess.

'I brought them back with me,' she said, as though the
portrait were her most treasured possession.

Once removed, my boots steamed in the hearth.

Martha sat in the chair opposite me.

I wished Mary Latimer would come closer, but I saw it
was part of her plan to remain briefly apart from us.

'Were you ever here before?' Martha asked me.

'No, never.'

'And were you never here during the summer?'

'This is my first visit.'

'Mine, too. I did once know a girl who lived here, but
this is my own first visit in so many years. It was a much

larger place then, of course.' There was seeming contradiction in everything she said.

'It was never larger than this, Martha,' Mary Latimer said. 'We have merely retreated, cave-dwellers that we have become, to the only remaining habitable rooms.'

'Have we? Will we get it all back?'

'One day. Perhaps.' She at last came to join us.

Martha occupied herself by inspecting my boots and moving them away from the heat of the fire. I saw Mary Latimer surreptitiously hold the hem of her sister's dress away from the mound of glowing embers as she did this.

'Will you take tea, Mr . . .' She had forgotten my name.

'Weightman.'

'Of course. Mr Weightman.'

I said I would, but rather than prepare this, she simply sat and looked at me.

'She baked a cake,' Mary Latimer said to me. 'Flour and water. No yeast, no sugar, no butter. Flat as a discus and hard as stone.'

Then Martha looked at her sister and said, 'We'll take tea. Attend to it, please.'

Mary Latimer curtsied and said, 'Yes, ma'am.'

When she was out of the room, Martha lowered her voice and said to me, 'She bakes, but the results are awful. You may have to eat something just to show willing.'

I entered into the conspiracy and promised her I would. After that she sat in silence until her sister returned. There was something about her which reminded me fleetingly of my several indulgent spinster aunts when I was a child, tolerant beyond duty, and then silent when their indulgence finally reached its limit.

Upon Mary Latimer's return a distinct and unpleasant odour followed her in from the adjoining room.

'You'll have to ignore it,' she said, indicating her sister, who now busied herself with the cups and saucers set down beside her. Only she seemed oblivious to the foul smell.

'She knew you were coming. I told her often enough. I went out briefly.'

'What is it?'

'She's boiling blackthorn.'

'Blackthorn? Is it a medicine, something to drink?' Among the houses lower down I had occasionally seen the slopes arranged with tenter racks. 'Is it a dyestuff?'

Mary Latimer signalled for me not to persist with my questioning. On her knees between us, her sister poured the tea and handed each of us a cup and saucer and spoon. I expected the fragile crockery to betray some infirmity or shaking, but there was none. Even the surface of the liquid itself was flat and undisturbed.

'You might come another day and I would spill it all down you,' she said, her tone even and serious. She sat beside me, her hand on the arm of my chair. 'It was good of you to come and see us,' she said.

'I would have come eventually as part of my work here.'

'To drive us out and let the water come.'

'Martha, Mr Weightman—'

'Was it you who drove out the girl who once lived here?' I looked to Mary Latimer.

'This is Mr Weightman's first visit to the valley, Martha.'

'He already told me that.' Her confusion grew more apparent, and with it she grew frustrated. She behaved like a woman who could remember and understand only the very last thing she had been told.

Mary Latimer understood this only too well. It was why she repeated the same few details over and over. Perhaps it was even why she insisted on repeating her sister's name each time she spoke to her.

'And how are we to go on living here?' Martha said.

'We won't. I doubt if the house will even—'

'Not the house,' Martha said. 'The water.'

'The water?'

'How are we to go on living here when everything is water?'

The question dismayed me and I considered how best to frame my answer.

'Say nothing,' Mary Latimer told me, her concern turning to amusement. 'She's teasing you.'

The woman beside me laughed at the trick she had played on me. Her laughter grew loud, and then louder still, and she clasped herself and rocked in childish delight.

Mary Latimer let this continue for a short while and then went to her sister and held her. The laughter subsided and the rocking ceased. Eventually the woman sat silent and motionless.

'Your tea,' Mary Latimer said to her, putting the cup and saucer back in her sister's hands.

Martha looked hard at what she now held, but made no attempt to raise the cup to her lips.

I sensed that a boundary had been crossed, and that as a consequence of this my presence now made Mary Latimer feel uncomfortable.

Accordingly, I retrieved my still-steaming boots and told her I would go.

She acknowledged my understanding with a nod.

'But where will we live?' the woman sitting beside me

suddenly shouted, great violence in her voice. 'He hasn't said where we will live. Why doesn't he tell us?'

Mary Latimer came again to hold her.

I pulled on my boots and went outside to lace them. Mary Latimer came out to me a moment later.

'I'm sorry,' she said.

'Please, don't apologize.'

'No, I'm sorry for myself. I would have liked you to have stayed longer. We could have talked.'

The house behind us was silent.

'Will she be all right?'

'She already is. I think perhaps there was too much for her to take in. At least you didn't have to eat the cake.'

'And the blackthorn?'

She hesitated before answering, breathing deeply, and even there, outside, catching some faint odour of it.

'When we were children, some of the girls we associated with, daughters of our tenants, our hired help, they used to boil the wood in the belief that it stemmed their bleeding.'

'Their bleeding? You mean when they were injured?'

'For some reason, Martha remembered. All her time in Colne and elsewhere, she never forgot.'

'I still don't—'

'Their monthly bleeding. The girls thought that by drinking the infusion they could somehow stem or reduce their bleeding.'

Only then did I understand what she was telling me.

'She may occasionally forget my name, her own even, but some things . . .'

I told her not to explain.

'I couldn't,' she said simply.

A cry from inside the house distracted us both. Martha stood at the window waving out at us.

'She's waving at you,' Mary Latimer said.

I returned the gesture, and the instant I did so, the woman at the window ceased.

18

I was woken late the following morning by a man at once banging on my door and shouting up at my window. I woke with a start, unable to locate the source of this racket. I lay fully dressed, my bedclothes on the floor. Whoever had come to rouse me moved from the front of the house to the back, where he knocked and shouted again.

Rising, I doused my face and went down to him. I imagined he had brought me some communication, and I could see how this might be considered an event of some note, warranting his clamour.

He was standing before the door as I opened it, and he considered me for a moment without speaking as I fastened up my coat. I recognized him and asked him what he wanted that was so urgent. One of my buttons was missing.

I remained unshaven, my hair uncombed, and my appearance made him apprehensive. I asked him again what he wanted.

'The water,' he said.

'Has something happened? Has someone been injured?'

He then composed himself, suddenly conscious of his duty and his role in the proceedings. 'A maelstrom,' he said.

'A what?'

'A maelstrom.'

'Do you mean a whirlpool?'

'A maelstrom.' He nodded vigorously to give emphasis to the word.

I rubbed the last of the sleep from my eyes.

'A maelstrom has formed in the rising water.'

'Where?'

'The river has flowed over its old course and a maelstrom has formed.'

'Stop using that word. We are not sailors caught in an Atlantic gale.'

His face dropped in puzzlement.

'Where?' I said again.

'Beneath the chapel. You must come and see.' He reached out, as though to grab my arm, but then thought better of the gesture and took back his hand.

'I must do no such thing,' I said, knowing immediately that it was my duty to go.

'And bring all your tools. And your books for writing down.'

'Do you know the cause of the pool?'

'Only the Lord himself—'

'Knows the answer to that. Of course.'

He considered me coldly. The door behind me swung on its hinges. I told him to come inside and wait, but he declined, saying he would wait for me where he stood. Then I told him to return to the site of the pool and wait for me there, but he refused to do that too, insistent on accompanying me, and no doubt wanting to herald my arrival and encourage further, endless speculation. The Lord was to have His day in the pool beneath the chapel.

Half an hour passed before I considered myself sufficiently presentable and went back out to him.

I cannot deny that my own excitement grew the closer we approached to the chapel. The usual small crowd was already in attendance. One man held a banner which he waved from side to side above his head. My guide and trumpeter pointed all this out to me. I told him I was neither blind nor deaf, and he looked at me as though waiting for me to present evidence to that effect.

Throughout our conversation he called me 'mester'. It is a hybrid of a word, born of and meaning both master and mister and all points in between. The scope of its additional meanings, twisted one way or another by the slightest inflection, was limitless. It might mean a dozen different things in the course of a single conversation from the lips of one man, depending on how he feared or favoured you in your dealings with him. Written down, the word acquits itself of all bias by being spelt 'maister'.

I paused on a small rise overlooking the river. My guide came back to me and urged me on. I told him there was no urgency and took out one of my notebooks. I sketched a simple plan of the river and its flood plain below the chapel, including the recently covered fields and the widening bulge of the flow itself. I marked the date – the first of November – and this seemed somehow propitious to me. Below me, rumour and supposition had birthed a cataclysm which could not be ignored. I even imagined I could hear the singing of some apocalyptic hymn as I made my few simple notes.

I descended the final slope, and my companion ran ahead of me, pushing through the crowd with his torch of news. I had taken the precaution of wearing my rubberized boots, and as I arrived at the first of the spectators I pulled these up over my knees and shook loose the straps by which they were fastened. I heard words of admiration from some of the men I passed.

I stopped at the edge of the water and asked loudly to be told what was happening. My guide ran back to me, but I silenced him and asked for an explanation from someone else.

A woman came to me leading a goat. 'A maelstrom has formed in the lost river,' she said. 'My animal here was almost drowned.'

I waited for her demand for compensation.

'But fortunately you rescued it,' I said. I asked her to show me the pool. I had examined the river on my descent and had seen nothing out of the ordinary there.

The woman pointed over the calm surface. 'Be patient,' she said. The people around us fell silent. We stood like that for a full minute and nothing happened. As I watched, I tried to remember the configuration of the river and its banks beneath the still surface. It was neither particularly deep here, nor fast-flowing; there was no sunken building which might have collapsed to cause the disturbance. And nor, as far as I could remember from my charts, were there any air shafts or abandoned workings beneath the fields on either side.

The disappointment grew around me and a murmuring arose. I started to speak to the woman, but she waved me to silence. Her own gaze remained fixed on the water.

'There,' she said eventually, and slowly raised her arm to point. Her quiet word was amplified by others.

I looked out to where she pointed and saw that there was just then some disturbance on the surface of the water. A circle formed, running in a clockwise fashion, and made all the more noticeable by the configuration of flotsam which followed its course and gave emphasis to its design. The ring was eight or nine feet in diameter, and slow-moving, though with an appreciable increase in speed as it progressed. The motion was at its most violent towards the outer edge. The centre, the vortex of all this activity, remained relatively calm, though even there a definite swirling could clearly be seen developing. The cries from the onlookers grew louder.

'Well?' the woman beside me said. She looked from my face to my boots.

I guessed the water to be no deeper than two feet, reckoning this by the height of the walls against which it lapped. In truth I would have preferred to have waited before wading in and making my inspection, but the woman prodded me into action with another of her 'well's.

I occupied myself by raising and then lowering my straps, by loosening and then tightening my belt.

After several minutes of violent spinning, the whirlpool decreased in intensity, lost its power and faded. The circle of cut grass on its surface lost definition and again aligned itself to the flow of the submerged river.

I handed over my bag to the woman, and she looked at me as though I were about to embark on a long and uncertain journey. I would wade no more than twenty yards out and twenty yards back. She seemed about to speak to me – I wished she had – but remained silent. I had arrived, I had taken charge, I was taking action, and I would have appreciated some public recognition of this other than the brief cessation of murmuring which accompanied my first few steps into the treacherous depths.

The ground beneath the surface was softened, but otherwise good. A man stood beside me holding a rope. He offered this to me but I declined, pointing out to him the shallowness of the water into which I was wading. It surprised me to see how quickly most of them now disregarded or had forgotten what lay beneath the surface, imagining depth where none existed, and suspicious of something which had been exposed to plain sight only a few days earlier.

The man with the rope called me a fool. The word made me feel brave. I had become a man of action, and what I did that day would be remembered.

'If you see the maelstrom start to reappear,' I called out, 'then shout and let me know.'

I was answered by a dozen nodding heads and fearful glances.

'You'll know soon enough,' the man with the rope said, deflating my bravado.

I felt for the first time the weight of the water over my feet.

'Shout all the same,' I said to him. I wanted him to remain where he stood with his rope. I wanted him to stand ready to throw it out to me.

I waded further, until I was midway between the water's edge and where the pool had briefly formed. I moved more cautiously as I approached its lost centre, bracing myself against its sudden resurgence. But I felt nothing. The water rose to my shins and then to my knees. I calculated that I was now walking on the river bottom. I could feel its stones beneath my feet. I turned back to the watching crowd. The man with the rope raised it to me.

'Nothing,' I shouted. I raised my arms and turned in a full circle, an awkward dance of seeming nonchalance.

It was as I waded back and forth over the site of the pool that I felt a stronger current against my legs. I stopped moving and steadied myself. I looked down, searching around me. Someone on the bank shouted. I felt a ripple against the backs of my legs, and the floating grass again began to form itself into a pattern as the tow increased in strength and I moved my feet further apart to stand into it. I saw the circle form around me. The voices on the bank grew louder. Someone called for me to save myself, which I appreciated greatly, concentrating hard on avoiding the indignity of being knocked over in two feet of water and sitting in it up to my waist.

I saw that I was standing at the outer edge of the spinning pool, where the tug was strongest, and I managed by several judicious, shuffling steps to move myself towards its centre, where the current, though still appreciable, was much weaker.

'He moves to its centre,' I heard someone cry out.

I saw how impressive my action looked. 'Pray for me,' I called out. I raised my own clasped hands.

It sounded good to hear my voice above the clamour, and I wished the water itself could have made more of an effort on my behalf. Sure of my footing – if anything, the flow was already starting to fall away – I rocked from side to side, as though struggling against the current, and held out my arms to balance myself.

'It grows stronger,' I shouted. But I shall beat it. I did not shout this, but it was what I wanted clearly understood.

I could still not account for the phenomenon, other than to think that some lost or forgotten shaft or vent had been flooded and was now allowing the gathering water to some-how drain away, creating this surface disturbance. And I could not account for the intermittent nature of the occurrence other than to suggest that perhaps some buried blockage was being periodically shifted or cleared with the build-up of water above it. The Board would require my reasoned guesses, and I made them all as the water flowed and eased around me.

A few seconds later and my moment of glory had passed.

'It weakens,' I called out when the decreasing flow would have been obvious to all on the shore. I made a motion with my hands as though I were hastening it away.

Then I turned back to the crowd and moved slowly towards them. The man with the rope had discovered his own reserve of bravery and now stood up to his ankles in the water.

Disappointingly, the onlookers dispersed ahead of me. I had endured and ended their drama. My messenger led away the man with the banner, and I found my bag on the grass where the woman had been standing. Only the man who held the rope approached me and quizzed me on what I had seen, but he too seemed disappointed that there had not been some more dramatic conclusion to the morning's events, and as I struggled out of my boots he told me at great length about the other pools on each of the chief rivers into which all flotsam, living and dead, was drawn, never to be seen again. Perhaps they had hoped for something similar of their own.

19

My work today kept me out until after dark. Just as there are places in the far northern latitudes which remain light throughout the nights of high summer, so it seems to me that there are now days here when the covering of cloud from dawn to dusk gives the impression of night never having fully withdrawn.

Winter, I am told, will come in a succession of testing, exploratory jabs, usually late in the days and during the hours of darkness, and at decreasing intervals. And following these jabs, almost as though the season were aware of the preparations being made in advance of its final approach, it will make its hard and unyielding thrust into the stone and the air of the place. There are weeks at the turn of the year when the temperature seldom rises above freezing, and when sheets and teeth of ice persist throughout.

I have seen the moon shining as bright at three in the afternoon in a broken sky as at three in the morning when I have woken and looked out. My bedroom is bathed in its cold light, penetrating the curtains and casting its grid of small frames over my bed and the wall beside.

I returned home earlier along the mine road and saw in the darkness how the pale stones set into its surface created a luminescence and gave it the appearance of a river flowing in the moonlight.

Earlier still, while out surveying, I saw in the distance beyond the dam the trail of steam rising from a passing engine. The machine itself I neither saw nor heard – the wind was behind me – but its plume of white I saw clearly enough, unravelling above the woodlands and cuttings through which the track ran. It surprised me to see it so close – though in truth it was still eight miles off.

I have packed torn rags into the door and loose window frames. Locally, the householders boil lumps of coal in their kettles and somehow manage to keep alight the gases rising from the spouts. I have experimented with producing my own gas, but with no success. There is always too much steam to kill the flame, and what little I do manage to boil off and keep alight fills the room with its stink rather than its glow.

I have taken a cold after my exertions, and suffer from a headache and a nausea that my volatile does little to alleviate. I am loath to use my common remedy so soon. And, in truth, it is of course no remedy, merely a means of alleviating the symptoms of an illness otherwise known as misery, touching at times on despair.

Afterwards, I sat in my swaddle of blankets and looked at her likeness – it is all I possess of her now – until I found myself close to weeping. By which, of course, being a man, I mean that I wept.

20 _____

For the first time, my work took me into the abandoned quarry and stone-yard. Hewn and uncut slabs lay all around the workings, affording me some impression of the activity in the place on the day when someone, calculating that sufficient rock had been cut and shaped for the dam, blew his whistle and shouted to everyone working there that their labour and pay were finished.

The blocks and splinters of rock amid which I stood were vividly red on their cut surfaces, and the low sun brightened these even further. I tried to climb several of the mounds, but was defeated by their looseness, making the noise of ten men in my clumsy attempts.

All the cutting and drilling machinery had long since been removed, and would no doubt now be at work elsewhere as the Board's schemes fed one upon the other and leapfrogged into the future.

It was as I returned to the quarry entrance that I saw Mary Latimer walking alongside the river below me. I watched her for a moment to ensure she was alone. Had her sister been with her, I would not have revealed myself to them.

Upon seeing me, she stopped walking and I made my way down to her.

'I was examining the quarry,' I said.

'Before it was excavated for the dam there was a cave which was once home to a hermit.'

I had heard of such a thing only once before. The estate owner of the village in which Helen had lived had, during the summer months when his house and lands were frequently visited, employed the services of a man to sit in a grotto with a candle in one hand and a Bible in the other. For a few coins he would read to his small audiences. I visited the place once with Helen and her sister. He was a civilized hermit and read well, and because of this I was disappointed by him, by the sham he had allowed himself to become.

'It was said he was able to cure most ailments by the laying on of hands.' Mary Latimer spoke almost in a reverie, and I saw again how tightly the vine of her sister was wound through and around her.

'And *were* people cured?'

'I doubt it. But they came. He lived on their charity. I remember being told by my grandfather that he was some harmless lunatic driven away from other places and that he had come here in torment to purge himself in his miserable isolation.' Her casual use of the word 'lunatic' surprised me and she saw this. 'Then, as now, it seems, we lived in an endlessly scrutinizing and judging age.'

'Did your sister recover after my visit?'

'Rest assured, you were quickly forgotten. My grandfather said the man absorbed all the sicknesses that were visited upon him into his own body and that he sat alone with them, making no attempt to cure himself until they left him of their own accord and he made his recovery. This was never a healthful place. Dysentery, diphtheria, the smallpox, other small plagues; that is what they were called. I don't know how long the man persisted, two or three years perhaps, but to survive even that short time through the winters here was a miracle of sorts, I suppose.'

'What became of him?'

'I don't know. I remember that after a year or two he was visited more frequently, that people came from elsewhere to seek his help. Most, I imagine, were simply curious, pleasure-seekers after some new novelty, come to scoff at him. But some were kinder. Some came to talk to him, brought him food. He held a great fascination for children.'

'So did you and your sister visit him?'

She paused at the memory. 'Must you endlessly have your connections, Mr Weightman, however tenuous?'

'It wasn't my intention to suggest—'

'I know. But you see how adept I have become at seeing these things and avoiding them. Yes, she and I came here. It seemed a strange place, then, before the quarry, before the river was lowered; strange and isolated, even by the standards of the valley.'

'Do *you* think he was a lunatic?'

'Possibly. But a harmless one. Perhaps just a soul provoked beyond endurance.'

'As you are now provoked by my own prodding.'

She looked beyond me into the derelict workings. 'I daresay if he had been more provoked or ridiculed then there were other, even more distant and unvisited places for him to have lived.'

'Then he was no Paul of Thebes, your hermit.'

She laughed. 'No, nor an Antony of Egypt come to us on a quest for the spiritual alembic from which he would emerge purified and beatified.'

'Ah, then if there is any connection between the man and the present place, then it is between him and me.'

She laughed again at this. 'You are no hermit, Mr Weightman, merely alone and lonely and a very long way from where you think of as home. You expected much more, and everything you are now forced to confront here only disappoints you further.'

The words struck me like blows, and I could not understand how we had come so swiftly from one path to the other. She saw their effect on me and reached out, as though she were about to touch me and comfort me.

'I don't deny any of it,' I said.

'But it was still unthinking of me to have put it so bluntly. I apologize.'

I turned away from her, back to the quarry. 'My employers are worried about the effect of so large and deep a structure on the flow beneath the dam.'

Water was already being released to provide for those manufactories and other concerns downriver which had come to private terms with the Board to maintain their own supplies. It was something I had hoped not to have to explain to her, being yet another weight placed upon the scales of loss and gain, where the loss was all here and the gain all elsewhere.

'Excavate a new channel,' she said. 'Make simple that which others strive to complicate.' Then, in a further gesture of reconciliation, she said, 'Martha was speaking this morning about Noah's ark. I imagine others have already made some comparison.'

'What would I take? Sheep, rabbits, crows? Not much of a new beginning.'

'No. But it was comforting to me to hear her talk about it. Another of your connections.'

'She must have understood or remembered sufficient of my visit, of why I am here, to have raised the subject.'

'Yes. She occupied herself by making a list of all you would need.'

'I daresay there are others here who would be only too happy to assist her.'

'And who would then draw up the gang-plank and bar your entry as you approached through the rising water.'

'It seems a fitting enough punishment for all I have destroyed here, for the Perpetual Spring I have ended.'

'I have to return to her,' she said.

You are as lonely and as alone and as disappointed as I am. It was beyond me to even suggest the thought. Unnecessary, also, for her own understanding of these things – of what she called my 'connections' – far surpassed my own.

She shook my hand and then returned to the river-bed below. She was lost briefly in the impenetrable shadow of the dam, but then I watched as she re-emerged on the far bank. I waited where I stood, but it was her habit, once walking, neither to pause nor to look back.

I made my own way homewards after that, searching

around me for everything I had so far passed unseen. I added sparrows and starlings and mud-caked pigs to my list of saved creatures. A fluttering white dove, I saw, would have been asking the impossible.

It was dark before I reached my door. Lights like the glowing bodies of insects drifted along the path beneath me, and, high above, patches of starlit sky were fleetingly revealed to me amid the coursing night cloud.

Part Two

21

I have made my first significant error. I daresay there have been inadvertent others – countless small miscalculations and misjudgements that the rising water has quickly erased, leaving that mirror in which only perfection is reflected – but I call this the first of my significant errors – perhaps 'deceit' would be more honest – because I was complicit in its making, by which I mean it was the result of a decision on my part where other, more honest courses still remained open to me. I acknowledge it here, though I daresay, like all those other small failings, it will be ignored elsewhere, lost to the water like a splash and afterwards of no consequence whatsoever.

Following almost two months of weekly dispatches to the Board, I received a communication from them suggesting that all my various reports might be more easily understood and *appreciated* were they to be gathered together, abridged, and presented as an overview of the scheme as a whole. As a sop to my standards and dedication, however, it was suggested that the individual points of interest within these overviews might then be developed by me in greater detail, ready to be inspected should anyone reading the shorter summary wish to do so. I received this communication – only the second since my arrival here – following a long day's surveying, and it might easily be imagined how quickly my delight at seeing it on my floor turned to anger at its suggestions. I mention all this here only to make clear how unremarkable my error will remain and that it has acquired significance in my own mind only.

Five days ago I visited the far shore to determine the extent to which the streams debouching into the reservoir on that side were also depositing their silts into it, and also to see what new land was being claimed by the backing up of their courses. In my initial instructions it was pointed out to me that should any of these lesser courses be radically affected by blockage or change of direction as a consequence of the rising water, then conduit channels might afterwards need to be dug to cope with any wayward overflow. It was common practice elsewhere, especially where the slopes of the feeder streams were not so steep. It was also suggested that I pay particular attention to the faster-flowing tributaries which entered closer to the dam. These, I was unnecessarily reminded, carried the greatest load of silt, and this would be laid down in the deeper water against the foundations where the flow was at its slowest, allowing sediment to build up where it was least wanted.

I left early in the morning. The most direct route to have taken would have been to walk down to the houses and across the dam, thereby surveying the most important of the feeders first, afterwards crossing the lesser streams on a long walk back up the valley. But I chose to avoid the dwellings, and went instead to a point two miles above my house where the river, though now slowly widening, was still easily fordable. From there I turned downstream, making my notes, drawings and judgements as I went.

I was midway through my work when, fording a particularly stony tributary, I stumbled and twisted my ankle. The pain initially was severe, but quickly subsided. I took off my boot and bathed my foot in the numbing water. There was some bruising, but not much, and I soaked a handkerchief and bound my foot tightly. Replacing my boot, I rose and found that, though there remained some discomfort, I could still walk, and so I continued downstream.

After a further half-hour, however, the pain increased and it became clear to me that I would be unable to complete my survey. Nor, at that reduced pace, would I be home before dark. The cloud that day was dark and high, resembling beaten pewter, and the day remained cold.

An hour after my fall I found myself opposite my house. There was no longer a ford where I stood, but I knew that by switching from channel to channel and negotiating the low shoals between them I would be able to cross with the water no higher than my knees.

Upon entering it, however, I found the river to be faster and deeper than I had anticipated, and I made several miscalculations before reaching the far bank. The pain in my ankle was again considerably lessened by my long immersion. I sat on the bank and rubbed the feeling back into my calves.

After a short rest I resumed my journey. The climb exhausted me further and I paused frequently. Eventually, the pain became excruciating again, and the noises I made as I panted up the final yards to my door sounded more and more animal-like.

It was several hours before I was able to reapply a bandage and then contrive a soft slipper from sacking and twine in which to cushion my injury.

I slept well and woke late the following morning. The pain still lingered, but much decreased, and so long as I kept my weight from the injured foot I found I could move around easily with the help of a stick.

Because any further excursion was out of the question, I chose to continue with several unfinished reports, and to compile the one upon which I had embarked the previous day. I completed my observations on the streams I had visited. I predicted nothing that anyone in possession of an understanding of the situation would not also have predicted, but there was substance to the work; it revealed the expertise of a man familiar with his enquiry; there was a measure of pride involved.

And then I grew frustrated that the report must remain of necessity incomplete, that its most significant part – the streams closest to the dam – must remain excluded. By early afternoon I had come to a standstill. I did not want to return to my other outstanding work, and so instead I went on with my report to include the tributaries I had not visited.

I did not allow myself to become over-imaginative in my fabrications; I merely addressed each stream through an understanding of its morphology, its flow and its gradients, and made predictions which, eventually, the rising water would allow to be neither proved nor disproved.

22 _____

'When we were girls we were occasionally allowed to accompany our father on his business trips to what seemed to us then the most distant places. We went with him to Leeds and York, Richmond and Darlington. We even went with him once to Carlisle and Whitehaven.'

'What business was it?'

'I cannot say for certain. Except that in addition to his doctoring he had some interest in several pharmaceutical firms. Knowing him even as I did then, I imagine he took his duties seriously. Perhaps he travelled to attend meetings. Perhaps he travelled only to be somewhere other than here. My mother was firm that she would not accompany him – I think that perhaps she alone saw the folly in all this moving around – but she was gracious enough to allow Martha and myself to go with him. They were such great adventures for us. We stayed in hotels, and in boarding houses on the way. I think I knew even then that I would not remain here, would not live here for ever.'

'And Martha?'

'She was always more of a home-bird. She relished the travelling to begin with, but as she grew older – remember, she cannot have been much older than eleven or twelve when all this started – she declined more and more often to come with us.'

'And so you accompanied him alone.'

'I did. And they were the most memorable occasions of my young life. Do you remember your own father well?'

I told her that I did, even though he had died when I was sixteen. She heard the reluctance in my voice and did not pursue the matter.

We stood at the door to her home. It was a clear day and there was some real warmth in the sun where we faced it. We turned into it and closed our eyes against its brilliance, as though we were lizards or some other cold-blooded creatures dependent on it for our energy. We both knew these were rare days, soon gone.

Martha stood at a short distance from us. She washed clothes in a bowl and then wrung these out, making a pool at her feet. I had spoken to her upon my arrival and she had seemed lucid and clear-headed. She had told me the whereabouts of her sister and returned to her work.

'Did these early travels encourage you to look beyond this valley, once you were grown?'

'They let me know that I would not remain, that I would take my chances elsewhere.'

'So only Martha chose to stay?'

'While that opportunity remained to her, yes.'

'I spoke to her earlier,' I said. 'Her mind seemed clear.'

She held my arm and led me away from the other woman until we were beyond the dilapidated garden wall and in the taller grasses beyond.

'I was always my father's favourite,' she said. 'He was a fair man and he treated us both well and equally, but there was no denying that he preferred my company over Martha's.'

'You were the elder,' I said. 'You better understood him.'

'Martha attached herself to our mother. After a year or two of joining us on our travels, she refused to go anywhere at all. She made this place her world. There was considerably more land then, and it was still good. It was the world she knew, the world she grew up imagining she would inhabit. She grew in accordance with all these expectations.'

'Whereas you cut yourself free of them.'

'Severed myself. I did. And with no expectation of coming back except to visit. I imagine Martha and my mother believed I had ideas above my station in life.'

'And only your father encouraged you in your plans.'

'He knew that I would never be contented here, that the longer I imagined myself restricted to the place, the harder I would pull to leave it and the further I would eventually go upon my release.'

'Did your mother see what you wanted?'

She pushed back the loose hair from her forehead. 'She acquiesced to his wishes. It created some conflict between them, and I regret that to this day.'

'And between Martha and yourself, I imagine.'

She turned to look at me. 'Light and bushel, Mr Weightman.'

'It was a guess, but I can see how such conflict might arise. People change, they grow apart, their ambitions divide and oppose.'

'She thought I should make a good marriage here. You would not think it to look at the valley now, but thirty years ago, less, it was a prosperous place. The manufactories were coming closer. There was even talk of laying a permanent road over the valley top. A branch line was proposed that would bring the railway to within half a mile of the village.'

I saw how unlikely this ever was to be realized, what labour and expense would be involved for little return.

'It was only when neither of these projects came to anything that the place began to suffer. The workplaces came only so far, and then they stopped, failed and withdrew. Better sites elsewhere, I suppose. And for all those years before your water, the place languished. There was always some great thing about to happen here, always some unlikely fortune about to be made.'

'But by then you were far away from it.'

'And both my parents dead and Martha in the asylum, yes. I wonder if you can conceive of a collapse of expectation on such a scale and with such consequences. Everything, everything we had held dear, all those childish certainties to which we had clung for so long, all of them taken away from us.'

'Which is why it will not grieve you so greatly to see the place finally flooded and lost for ever.'

'And why Martha will grieve for it so much more intimately.' She folded her arms and held them tight across her chest.

'My father had his own shipping company,' I said. 'I imagine he always assumed I would take it over from him. In his youth he was often at sea. He travelled frequently between London, Liverpool and Bristol. His father and grandfather before him made the firm the success it was. He, too, suffered reverses.'

'Did you disappoint him greatly?' she said.

'I imagine so.' It was still beyond me to tell her about my mother.

At that point, Martha appeared around the side of the house, shielded her eyes to search for us, and then called to us. She shook her hands dry as she came and rolled down her sleeves. The ground between us was marshy and she diverted left and right to remain on the drier parts.

'He would have drained and improved it all,' Mary Latimer said, meaning her father. I saw how sustaining her memories of the man remained to her. And I saw too how she kept him to herself, how Martha's own, imperfect recollections were kept apart.

Martha joined us.

'I was calling for the horses,' she said. She looked around us. 'Have you seen them, Mr Weightman? Did you pass them on your way up here?'

'Horses?'

'I let them graze over the hill, Martha,' Mary Latimer said, her eyes on mine.

'I thought we might go for a drive in one of the carriages,' Martha said.

'Later, perhaps.'

'Will you accompany us, Mr Weightman? Or perhaps you would prefer to take us out on the lake in a boat.'

'Nothing would give me greater pleasure,' I said, looking to the other woman to ensure I had said the right thing.

'You cannot swim,' Mary Latimer said.

'Me, neither,' I confessed.

'The sailor's respect for the sea?' Mary Latimer said.

'My mother considered me a weak and sickly child,' I said. 'A single drop of water might have killed me.'

Martha stared at me as I spoke, as though fascinated or alarmed by what I said. Then her reverie broke and she abruptly turned and left us. She started calling for the horses and clapping her hands to summons them.

Mary Latimer left me, and keeping her guardian's distance from her sister, went after her.

23

It was in the company of the men of the Board that I first saw a map of the scheme in its entirety. The word 'scheme' was theirs; here, as elsewhere, it retains its more obvious meanings and associations and I avoid the use of it wherever possible in my dealings.

They unrolled their map like the treasure chart it was. The blank high land they had shaded the palest ochre, more yellow than brown, and they had removed from the map all those features which did not concern them, erasing both history and geography in this newly drawn world of theirs. In this sense, as in others, they truly were the Lords of Creation. The water – or, as I saw it more prosaically denoted, 'supply' – they had coloured the brightest of blues. A blue unseen beyond paintings of the sunlit

Mediterranean. A lake beyond lapis lazuli, beyond azure, and already with the appearance of being a perfectly natural feature, more recorded than predicted or ordained. I saw how simple and yet how all-consuming and convincing a deceit they had created.

And, as with the empty spaces of the ochre moors, so everything that might once have existed beneath the level of the coming water was also expediently removed. Thus were loss and change erased and abridged.

The few dwellings which did survive the map-drawing stood like ornamental lodges or boathouses along the shore of the lake. The blue threads of the tributaries remained in place, as did the river flowing from the base of the dam. In fact, the only unnatural-seeming feature on the whole chart was the dam itself, and even here their imaginative map-maker had sought to disguise its outline by thinner lines than elsewhere and by the drawing of dense woodland – in reality thin, dying trees – at either end of the wall.

The map impressed me. How could it do otherwise? That was its purpose. That was the intention of the men who had invited me into their comfortable company and then shared with me this secret of the future. I was their honoured guest, and I displayed all the appropriate surprise and appreciation. And while I studied those blues and yellows they asked me if I still considered myself to be the man for the job, and like any man thus flattered and rewarded in conspiracy, I was beyond all denial or refusal.

I remember now that amid my ball of thoughts on that occasion was the recollection of a distant memory when, as a boy, I had been shown a map of the Guinea coast bought by my father at an auction room in Winchester, upon which was printed the repeated warning 'Cannibals: No Fresh

Water Here'. My father had seemed no less thrilled than I had been to discover the wording and all it implied. And perhaps because of that simple connection so forcibly made, I knew as well as any of those men of the Board that the job they offered me was mine.

I see now – just as assuredly as I was blind to it then – how considerably less appealing to the shareholders and investors a chart coloured the true colours of the gathering water under these dark hills and skies would have been.

I had enquired if I might bring with me a copy of the map with which to impress anyone who came to ask me about my work, but they had refused me without explanation, and had afterwards treated me as though I had betrayed a confidence to which we had all been sworn.

24

Two hundred years ago, according to local legend – it is that genus of story – a woman was forcibly drowned in a pool beneath one of the river's bridges, and the stones of the structure were afterwards pulled apart and cast into the water to cover her where she lay and to conceal the crime of her murder.

I heard the story, ever varying in its finer details, from several tellers. I learned the woman's name, that none of her descendants any longer lived there (they had all been driven away after the crime), that she had been killed by her husband, a hard-working, well-liked and respected local man, that she had been killed because of her unfaithfulness to him – and not merely that, but that she had been unfaithful to him with a gypsy man, and that she was also with child as a result of this alliance.

I saw in the story all the elements of a perfect tale, one changing in shape and colour and emphasis as it was told and told again.

I insisted on being shown where the drowned woman was buried, where the bridge had once stood that was now her tomb. Accordingly, I was taken to a place where the river-bed, divided into a dozen rising channels, did indeed seem mounded at its centre with dry boulders.

I knew of a number of processes by which such a feature might have come naturally into being, but I kept close counsel, and instead I remarked upon the impressive appearance of the tomb.

I asked if the stones had ever been investigated to see if the remains of a body lay within them, but here too the tale was sealed and protected by the dread and certain knowledge that were the dead woman's spirit to be disturbed, then something terrible would befall the valley and its people. The man who told me all this made no connection between this lurid curse and what was happening now, and I changed the subject to avoid the association being made in my presence. I also resisted the urge to suggest that perhaps the stones should be excavated before the grave was lost for ever, that this was now the only decent, the only *Christian* course to take. It was similarly beyond me to suggest that, in view of the present circumstances, the woman's tortured soul might now be released at no real cost to the valley or the people shortly about to leave it.

Of a bridge elsewhere in the valley, I had heard the story told in Halifax of how the owner of the structure had demanded to be paid extra for it once the price was fixed on his land. The Board refused and the man fought the case in a local court, but was ultimately defeated. The court spectators, apparently, had burst into laughter when one of the Board's lawyers, sensing victory, had asked the owner how much he believed an underwater bridge to be worth.

25 _____

Years ago – in that other life – walking alongside the lake with Helen, I saw the taking of a duck by a pike, which rose vertically from the water to appear at the surface with its jaws already fully extended and the duck already a meal. It was not a duckling of which I speak, but a grown bird, a female mallard. So sudden, so unexpected and clean was its seizure, that only a moment later, the ripples already dead on the otherwise calm surface, it was impossible for me not to already begin to doubt what I had witnessed, despite the evidence of my own eyes.

Helen, walking alongside me only a moment earlier, had paused and turned away from the water to gather some primroses which grew at the edge of the woodland there. I watched, mesmerized, as the fish rose out of the lake to its full, brilliantly green length, the duck already lost to its maw as it hung in the sunlight and the water drained from its flanks, and then as it twisted to one side, fell gracefully and with a loud slap and was even more abruptly gone. I was slow to gather my wits and call out, and when I did shout for Helen to come and see, all that remained of the fish and the lost bird was the barely disturbed surface of the water.

She asked me what I had seen, and I pointed and told her. She did not believe me, accusing me of having thrown a stone into the water. There were no other birds on its surface. We walked on a gravel path bordered by lawn; there were no stones large enough to make such a splash. Conceding this, she suggested that what I had seen had been a fish breaking surface and nothing more. I searched the water for some sign of what had happened – a feather, perhaps – but there was nothing. Then she suggested that a child hidden in the trees was playing a game with me, and she pointed to where the rhododendrons overhung the edge of the water, and where someone might easily have been hidden.

I remember I grew unaccountably angry at her refusal to believe me, and I became louder in my insistence until eventually she threw down the few flowers she had gathered, told me to believe what I liked, and then left me. She stopped after a minute's brisk walking and waited for me to catch up with her and apologize for my behaviour. Which is what I did. Which is what she knew all too well I would do. Her primroses lay unretrieved behind us, proof of my intransigence.

Our walk back to the house took us a full circuit of the small lake. It was late spring. Flies hatched on the water's surface, and were here and there immediately nibbled at by small fish, perhaps themselves only recently hatched. She saw this and indicated it to me. Her tone was now conciliatory, and at no point then did I question why she had chosen not to believe me and had sought for these other answers instead.

Martins swooped low out of the boathouse and these too scooped up the struggling flies. She pointed this out to me also. What I did later question was my own insistence at being believed. I behaved, I felt, like an innocent man unjustly accused of a crime.

As we neared the end of our walk, about to leave the lake and return to the lawn and the house, where others awaited us, there was a second large splash, but this time I saw only the aftermath of the disturbance and nothing of its cause.

It was at a greater distance from me than the previous splash, beyond one of the small jetties with its tethered boats, and I had been turned away from it when it had occurred.

I could already hear the voices of the others on the lawn, sitting at cane tables, spread on the grass, reading, talking, playing croquet. I remember I paused on the steps leading away from the water, and Helen said she hoped I was not going to delay. I assured her that I was not, my frustration and anger still thickly disguised.

She climbed the steps ahead of me. Two of her friends and her sister Caroline came forward to join her. I remained where I stood. Even in the sunlight, the water looked black beneath the trees.

'Charles saw a fish eat a duck,' I heard her say to them, her voice raised and incredulous. It was another of my punishments. The three other women called for me to tell them more.

'I threw a stick into the water some time ago,' one of them shouted. 'Perhaps it was that you saw.'

'See,' Helen said. She continued alone towards the house.

The others waited, watching me, whispering. I could distinguish their legs through the fabric of their dresses. They, too, had some notion of this, for they whispered more urgently and then ran away from me at my approach.

Ahead of them, Helen was now at one of the tables. The men around it turned their attention to her and my story skimmed the surface of the day.

Only Caroline came back to me. She was two years younger than Helen and I had a great affection for her. She held my arm.

'Why does she refuse to believe me?' I asked her.

'Because she knows, and tells everyone often enough, what a pedant you are.' I felt her grip tighten.

'Pedant?' I remember how the word dried in my mouth.

'She decries you because you believe only the evidence of your own eyes and understand only that which can be explained.'

'She says all this?'

We had been engaged to be married for almost a year, and here, already, was the first of those hairline fractures in the bowl through which the escaping water might one day begin its journey.

26 _____

'Will you tell me something about her, about you and her?'
I said.

'Something specific?'

'No, something of your past, of her illness.'

I had encountered Mary Latimer as I approached one of
my rain gauges. She stood beside the contraption and
raised her hand to me when I was still a great distance off.

I have three of the instruments, one on either side of the
valley and one on the old, diminishing flood plain. The
latter is frequently tampered with – filled on dry days,
emptied after storms – and I do nothing to deprive my
opponents of their small victories. I am a feeble wader in an
ocean of rain.

'She was first committed, not to any asylum, but to a

succession of nursing homes, when she was twenty-six. She was neither married nor engaged to be.'

'No suitors?'

'I was always considered the more valuable catch. No sons in the family. Our father owned land. In addition to being a doctor, he was also the local magistrate. No one could say for certain what caused her illness. All we knew – all *I* knew, for both our parents were dead before she finally stumbled and fell – was that she was happy and healthy and to all outward appearance fulfilled in her life before it happened.'

'Was nothing prescribed?'

'Rest, isolation, peace, quiet, diets, cures of water and air and inflated ideas.'

'So were you responsible for her, for her treatment?'

'Not entirely. I was married by then. My husband's business was in London. I visited her, of course, but, as you might imagine, her turmoil estranged us. Does it not seem callous to you for me to talk of events which took place over the course of twenty-five or thirty years as though they were the actions of an hour?'

'Did nothing help her?'

'It occurs to me now that we sought too hard, that there was never any 'cure', and that all we should ever have hoped for from the very beginning was for some inner calm or ease within her. When she was young she fought against the loss and the restraint of her life ahead.'

'And now?'

'Now you might say she is bound to the rock of acceptance. Perhaps I should have insisted on taking her to live with us.'

'Would that have been possible?'

'I'm afraid not. Neither my husband nor I had any true understanding of what was happening to her. How could we? All I knew was that I had lost my childhood companion and confidante to distant figures with their leeches and laudanum and blood-letting.'

'Were you concerned also that you too might become afflicted?'

'My honest answer, then, would have been yes. Or if not afflicted as such, then tainted by her madness.' She turned her attention to the contraption between us, hidden by the bracken. 'Our father was a man for the sciences in his own way. He knew Usher before he became a bishop and said he was the biggest fool he had ever met.'

'He was a firm believer in floods,' I said. I showed her the journal in which I kept all my recordings and observations regarding the rain.

'It is a thing he would have taken pleasure in doing,' she said. The simple association gratified her.

'Are your parents buried here?'

'In the chapel ground? No. There is a family plot thirty miles away. They were Quakers, or my mother was, and my father afterwards by conversion. He used to say that he was only truly woken to the love of God after his marriage.'

'Was it any comfort to you that they saw so little of what happened to their daughter?'

'None. After my departure, and for the short time left to them, they saw her frequently. They moved her from one place to another chasing her elusive cure. I visited her whenever I could, but I became a stranger to her. We retreated, I suppose, one from the other, and whereas I made a new life for myself amid everything I had ever wanted, all she found for herself was the unimaginable emptiness and darkness of her tortured soul. I make no apology for myself; I would be lying if I told you I did not understand all this as well – albeit imperfectly – then as now.'

She was distracted briefly and indicated to me far down the slope where a group of women had appeared, all carrying bundles of fuel on their heads, and giving themselves the appearance from that distance of giant mushrooms.

'Gathering dead stems,' she said. 'Kindling.'

'Most of them will soon be gone.'

'I doubt that has any bearing on how they will go on living here until the time comes.'

'Where was your sister prior to her return here?'

'Lancaster asylum. First Colne, then there. Have you heard of Samuel Morrison? An enlightened man. He was the first, it seemed to me – what little real interest I still showed – who understood what she needed. I was able to send money for her care. My husband was never less than generous where Martha was concerned. When the money was available to us, it was always forthcoming to pay for her special treatments and other comforts. A cynic might say it was sent out of conscience.'

For the whole four months of my own mother's stay in the sanatorium – I did not know then and I do not know now where it was located – she was visited by no one except my father on four separate occasions.

'And then, after a hitherto successful life in commerce, my husband suffered a succession of failures and unwise investments. Our small fortune evaporated. When he died I was forced to sell our home.'

'And return here?'

'Not immediately, no. I lived elsewhere, mostly on the

charity of friends. It was never my intention to return.
Upon our departure, our home here and the land attached
to it was let to a succession of tenants. I always anticipated
that it would simply crumble to dust if left empty long
enough. But I was still its owner, and when your masters
made their offer it was suggested to me by my parents'
solicitor that I ought to return, that by again taking up
residence here their offer might be increased. The solicitor
was convinced that they had no knowledge of who did or
didn't live in the house, of how worthless the land had
become. Was it a criminal or fraudulent thing to have
done?'

'Their offers started low and went down.'

'I know. I made the mistake of employing the man to
approach them and make an appeal on my behalf.'

The women beneath us were still within sight, but far
beyond our hearing.

'Did you think bringing your sister home would help
her?'

'No. I had known for some years that the situation – they
call it a 'regime' – at Lancaster had changed. Samuel
Morrison was replaced; his ideas were too revolutionary for
some. I learned how Martha was being treated there, how
she was being forced to live. I could no longer provide for
her. I went to visit her after an interval of almost a year. She
had changed so much, I could scarcely believe the
difference.'

'In what way?'

'I saw in her so little of what she had once been. Her
periods of clarity and understanding, which only a few
years earlier had lasted for days and weeks, were now
counted in hours, minutes even. But when I went to see

her she recognized me – spoke of countless remembered things – and before I left she begged me not to leave her there. You can see how circumstance conspired against me, from all directions, from above and below, and from inside as well as out. I might just as easily have gone to see her on a day when she would not have known me from a thousand others; I might have gone on a month of days when that was the case. But instead she knew me, and I knew her again, and I knew that regardless of my own circumstances, regardless of the countless other pleas I had thus far been able to ignore, it was beyond me to deny her now. She became very ill – influenza – after my visit and there was talk that she might not survive. Perhaps I imagined I was bringing her home to die. At best she might have survived a few weeks or months.'

'And be beyond all her suffering before the time came for you to leave.'

'It was always an imperfect plan. I make no excuses now for its failure.'

'Why? Because you cared for her and she recovered?'

'Because if I had thought about things properly I would not now be in the position of having to abandon her again.'

'Why must you?'

'Because someone here informed your masters that I was cheating them by having returned with her so recently, and that I had removed her from the asylum for that sole purpose.'

'They withdrew their offer of compensation?'

'Who would be so heartless? No, they merely reduced it and let me know that they would go on reducing it the longer I argued with them.'

'Can you not fight them?'

'You saw her, how she is. What am I doing but assuaging my own conscience by fooling myself into believing I can care for her? In addition to which . . .' She hesitated.

'Tell me.'

'In addition to which, my receipt of even the reduced compensation is conditional upon her removal. The relevant authorities, it seems, have been informed.'

I could not understand why she had not told me all this before.

'You must feel nothing but contempt for me,' I said.

'Why should I? You are to them and their water what I am to her and her treatment or care. We are watchers, you and I, Mr Weightman, observers, nothing more; we understand all the rules of engagement, but we are not participants.'

I could not accept the painful truth of what she was saying. I returned the phials I still held to their stand and let the lid of the gauge fall with a clap.

'If she were *your* sister, what would you do?' she said. 'I know it is an unfair question, but I am so *alone* in all of this that even its true injustice has no power to hurt me.'

'Where will she go?'

'Leeds.'

'And you?'

She shook her head. 'It is something I prefer not to think about until she has gone and I have convinced myself that there was nothing I could have done to prevent her going.'

'Have arrangements already been made?'

'Arrangements are always made. You of all people should know that.'

'Soon?'

'Soon enough.'

'Will you let me know if there is anything I can do?'

'You only say that because you understand your help-lessness in the situation as well as I understand my own.'

'I mean it,' I said.

She stood beside me for several minutes longer before holding out her hand to me and saying, 'And now, knowing all I have just told you, you will be left wondering which one of us to pity the most.'

27

Several days later, I was passing a group of resting miners on the mine road when I heard mentioned the name of the man Ellis, supposedly employed by the Board as bailiff, but who had still not yet made himself known to me.

Unlike most of the others, the miners had thus far kept themselves apart from me, and it occurred to me as soon as the name was mentioned that its purpose was to attract my attention.

There were seven men in all, and three boys, and the remains of a small fire smoked beside them.

I apologized for my intrusion, but even as I spoke they made way for me to sit among them. A piece of cloth as black as their clothes was laid down for me. Their skin, too, was picked out in its every crease and fold with dark lines, as though the men were plates etched with ink. Their teeth and eyes shone wet amid the darkness of their faces.

'I couldn't help overhearing . . .' I began.

'Ellis,' one of them said. 'Arrested in York.'

'Arrested?'

'Took all your employers' money and spent it.'

'He was paid to help me here.'

'We know he was.'

'Known him for ten years,' another added, his tone making clear to me their dislike of the man.

'What do you mean when you say "took"?'

'What I say. He was paid in advance to do a job. Took the money and threw it all away in York.'

'Why there?' I said.

'Perhaps he thought it was far enough away.'

The city was barely forty miles distant.

'There is a branch of the Board in York. They have several schemes connected with the place.'

'Bad luck on Ellis, then.' They all laughed at this.

'Is he in gaol?'

'Where he'll stay for six months until he's tried.'

'And in the meantime I am to go on without him.'

'Better off,' one of the older men said. He spat heavily into the cone of ash.

'I appreciate you letting me know,' I said.

I asked them their names. Most of the people here shared the same ten or a dozen Christian and surnames. As in all other things, there was no superfluity here, no exotic flowering amid the grasses and reeds. There were Riggs and Cloughs, Lumbs and Cleggs and Scales, all of which might just as likely have been the names of the features around them; thus were the two – people and place – bred into each other.

I was grateful for having been allowed so easily into their company and conversation. The rule here was to avoid whole sentences where a single word would serve, to avoid as many definite and indefinite articles as possible, and to eschew even words themselves where a grunt or a nod or a shake of the head was sufficient to impart the necessary meaning.

One of them handed me an enamel mug. I took it and drank from it, but what I had taken for water was a raw spirit and I choked at the sudden heat of it. The laughter of the men around me outlasted my coughing. I regained my breath and immediately the mug was refilled and handed back to me. I cannot deny that, though it was of the roughest sort, there was something satisfying about the numbing burn of that spirit, sitting on the cold hillside with only the prospect of another empty day and evening ahead of me.

I had heard it said of the miners that they drank copiously while they worked, and that working in a state of intoxication was the only way they managed to endure the extremes of their labour.

I asked them about the mines. A pipe was lit and handed round, coming to me in turn. They said the mines were played out and that they were excavating thinner and thinner seams. Only three small pits remained in operation. A decade ago there had been four times that number. The sale of the land alone had closed six mines. Some of the men had found work elsewhere; those who remained had taken over the workings from the old landowners. I could not begin to understand how they made them pay;

nor even how they transported their ore to the smelters so far away. I had some idea that this went over the valley head to the west, but I knew no more.

The mug was refilled several times over. I drank my share and we stayed like that for an hour.

When I finally came to stand I affected a greater sobriety than I felt. I had indulged myself in the ease of their company, and I took several deep breaths to clear my head. They themselves seemed little altered by the spirit; even the boys, who had taken their own lesser share, walked and talked without any obvious sign of it.

Our farewells were loud and prolonged.

28

I woke the next day still suffering from the drink, and I walked into the wind to clear my head. On the open land to the far north the heather was being burned in great swathes, filling the air with sheets of smoke.

I encountered an old woman following the course of the new shore. She came to where her path ran into the water and looked out over the unbroken surface.

'I wanted to see if the bridge was still there,' she said.

'Covered over,' I told her. 'Ten days ago was the last time any part of it showed. The water was at its foundations for a week before that.'

It had been the most substantial of the structures this far up the valley.

I looked around me. It was a rare, bright day, chilled but

with the illusion of warmth. Twelve years ago I had travelled in Greece, and I could not deny that there were similarities between this stony upland and some of the places I had visited then, and I was lost for a moment in my memories of the distant excursion. It had lasted almost three months, after which I was to set out and make my mark on the world.

There was a small but noisy rock-slide on the far side of the river and we both turned to watch as the loosened stones and turf slid into the water.

'We lived up at the head of the valley,' she said.

'Up here?' There was neither dwelling nor ruin to show where anyone might once have lived.

It was calm where we stood, but the wind could still be heard high above us. Tatters of cloud swept over the high tops, snagging and tearing where they touched.

Eventually she turned to me and put her hand on my arm.

'I saw that bridge being built as a child,' she said. 'My father and his brothers built it in a single day. There was never much water this far up, and many said there was no sense in building it. My mother was loudest of all in her complaints. They gathered the stones from these hills. He said the bridge would help him with his animals.'

'Then I'm sorry for its loss,' I said.

She went on as though I hadn't spoken. 'He carved his name, and the names of his wife and seven children in the stones.' She paused briefly. 'Shall I tell you why my mother was so against it being built? It was because she believed that malign spirits would not cross running water. Our house was on the far side. In her eyes, by building the bridge my father was doing nothing more than building a causeway for those dark spirits. Everyone else might have thought her stupid, but it was what she believed.'

'And she instilled that belief in you and her other children?'

'Don't be ridiculous. We live in the modern age. Look around you, the world is turning faster and faster. But I tell you this,' she went on, 'there are still those here who will spit three times before crossing the river. Even your dam won't cure them of that. When my father's bridge was built, people, small congregations, Rechabites and Antinomians from over the valley used to come and gather there. It became their pulpit, a place of baptisms, a gallery to stand and watch. If there are ever ghosts to come back and haunt this place, then it will be the joyless spirits of those Rechabites.' Then, pausing, and in a softer voice, she added, 'My mother washed the corpses of her five dead babies in this river, my brothers and sisters.'

'Is that why you came today?'

She nodded. 'And perhaps if the world had not been turning quite so quickly then I might have beaten it by those ten days and made my farewells properly.'

There was by then no limit to the losses to be endured, loss upon loss, and loss within loss, all of them as tangible now as a blighted crop rising from the desecrated land in which it had so long ago been sown and then forgotten.

29

I noticed how she held her hands, how she clasped the fingers of one in the palm of the other, and then deftly reversed the position. She saw me looking at this and immediately dropped her arms to her sides. A minute later, she was at this agitated clasping and squeezing again.

I asked her if there was no way she might calm herself.

For the first time in many weeks she had come to my lodgings. Martha had suffered a seizure the previous evening, and now, at dawn, the doctor had come, along with a woman to sit with her, and the two of them had sent Mary Latimer out of the house with instructions not to return for several hours.

I gave her a warm drink and built up my poor fire, pulling our two chairs closer to it.

Slowly, her anxiety subsided and she sat breathing deeply, as though she were coming to her senses upon waking.

'I'm pleased you came here,' I told her.

'I could think of nowhere else to go,' she said bluntly, then, catching my eye, added, 'Have I offended you?'

'Not at all.' I sipped at my drink and scalded my lips.

A fine, cold rain blew across the hills outside.

She put down her own cup and held her hands to the rising fire. 'I could have gone back to the dam, I suppose,' she said.

'Oh? Why there?'

'No reason,' she said. 'It seems to have become a focus for everything else that happens here, that's all.'

'I see.'

She looked slowly around the room. Her hands were again agitated in her lap. 'Fretting', they would call it here.

'Do they know what causes Martha's seizures?'

'They are common enough to most forms of madness, I believe,' she said. She remained distracted; other thoughts filled her head.

I took a deep breath. 'What would you have done if she had died? Or if the authorities had refused to release her into your care?' I said.

She smiled at my boldness. Her hands fell still and she pulled straight the material of her skirt.

'Would I have been grateful and relieved that the decision was no longer mine to make, its consequences no longer mine to bear alone, do you mean?'

I nodded.

'Had she died, I know I should not have let her be buried there. But if they had refused to release her to me, then I do not know. What do *you* imagine, Mr Weightman – would I have fought them, do you think? Or is that only what you might *want* to think of me?' She bowed her head. 'When she knows me and talks to me, when we share something together, something of what we were, then I am able to convince myself that what I did was for the best. But when, like last night, she raves at me and lashes out at me as though I were her vilest enemy, then I cannot convince myself that I would even want to know her as the most distant of my acquaintances. They tell me she is out of her mind at such times, but the things she recollects to throw at me, the things she says about me, about my treatment of her – I am less convinced than all those experts profess to be that the mad woman and the sane woman are as far apart as they insist.'

'Surely, there must be some common ground between the two states.'

'You sound like one of them.'

I sipped again at my drink.

'You say it, and because you believe it to be a reasonable and, in your eyes, valid explanation, you feel justified in having said it. But you are not there when all this happens. You stand on your clifftop and watch a storm far out at sea. There is a luxury in these explanations, in this easy knowing, that some of us are not afforded.'

I acceded to this in silence for several seconds. Then I said, 'But surely you must know that I am a man for whom not even the most violent of maelstroms holds any fears.'

She laughed. 'I heard. They are already saying you stirred up the water with your own feet and that you knew all about the phenomenon before you were called to tame it.'

I exaggerated my dismay at this dismissal of my bravery.

'What was the cause of it, do you imagine?' she said.

'Whatever it was, it was not what they would have wished it to be,' I said.

'A sea monster would have suited them best,' she said.

'I doubt any monster worth seeing would have possessed the courage to swim this far from the sea. In Halifax, the river is one day yellow, the next day purple, depending on what dyestuff they are using that day.'

'It would still have been something other than a dam and a reservoir,' she said.

'Is that why they were all so keen for me to wade out and investigate?' I said.

'You acquitted yourself well.'

'Only because I don't believe in monsters.'

'She was talking again yesterday, Martha, before her seizure, of the ark that someone somewhere might be building to save us all. We indulged each other in our speculation, and right up until the moment her eyes turned in her head and she fell from her chair, she was considering how such a thing might succeed. We decided eventually that however commodious and watertight a vessel might be constructed, there would be nowhere for it to go, nowhere for it to land and release its men and animals to begin anew.'

'So, the extent of my flood continues to disappoint,' I said. 'Do you believe all this excited imagining had anything to do with what happened afterwards?'

'I doubt it. She said I would not be allowed on board the ark because I was too old and too ugly and that no one would want me to bear their children. She, on the other hand, would be the most desirable woman there. She said every man in the valley would be competing for her. She rose to show off her figure, delineating point by point all this crowd of eager suitors might find attractive about her. I imagine she sought to embarrass me in some small and private way, but though I pretended to be shocked by what she said, I was, in truth, encouraged by it. She spoke as she had spoken as an excited girl with her life and her prospects still ahead of her. There was nothing truly salacious in what she said – just as there was nothing then, all those years ago – and she, too, revelled in her daring.'

'A pity then that the day did not have some calmer conclusion,' I said.

'A pity the water runs circles round you,' she said.

We sat together in silence for several minutes afterwards. The fire grew warmer, and the wind blew harder against the windows, adding to our illusion of warmth.

'Do they gather on the dam solely to condemn it?' I asked her.

'Whatever brings them to it, it's a hard thing to ignore. Did you imagine one or other of them might one day, and secretly, tell you that they admired it, that they saw in it what you see?'

'I thought their condemnation of it might not have been so unthinking, so . . . wholesale.'

'A man here might say he had heard a voice come down to him from a cloud and within a day fifty others would be ready to defend him against all detractors. And then the next day that same man might say something to offend one of those ardent defenders and all fifty would turn instantly against him and denounce him for what he foolishly imagined he had heard.'

'You think the men of the Board could have better paved my way here?'

'I don't see one single thing they have done to assist you except to stay away themselves. Where future schemes are concerned, I imagine your own role might be deemed superfluous by them. After all, you are the first to admit it – the dam is built, the water is coming, and nothing on earth will now alter that fact.'

'The dam might burst and the water race away faster than it came.'

'Whatever happens, it would still be too late for this place. The Book of Jeremiah, Mr Weightman. Chapter eight, verse twenty.'

I shook my head.

' "The harvest is past, the summer is ended, and we are not saved." '

' "Saved" from what? You embrace calamity where none exists,' I said.

'Them,' she said. 'Not me.' And with that she rose to leave me.

All the time she was with me, it later occurred to me, she had been aware in the acutest detail of everything that was happening to her sister on the far side of those hills.

I offered to accompany her home, and, as I anticipated, she refused. She said that my company would prevent her from ordering her thoughts. She said that the woman who had come with the doctor would remain with her, through the night if necessary. She did not tell me outright that she did not want me to go into that house with her and perhaps witness there what had been done to her sister.

'She may have made a full recovery,' she said to me, making no effort to convince me.

'I should like to return and see you both soon,' I told her, and thus bridged our two courses of evasion.

'I'm sure Martha would appreciate that.'

'Will you tell her?'

'Anticipation plays no part in any pleasure she might still experience.'

'I see,' I said. But I did not see. I did not see how one woman might know so precisely and so confidently the thoughts and imaginings of another.

She took my hands briefly in her own, before pulling tight her gloves and letting herself out into the wind.

30 _____

I sat today on the rise above the lower valley road and
watched a procession of those finally departing pass me by
below. Several families had hired horses and open carts to
transport their belongings. Furniture stood piled in
precarious mounds, rocking on the uneven road. Children
ran alongside. Others pushed their belongings on smaller
carts. I watched as one family took down a chest of drawers,
settled it carefully by the roadside and left it there.
Everyone coming behind stopped to inspect this. Several
drawers were taken out and salvaged. Other possessions,
mostly furniture, stood and lay scattered elsewhere.

I searched among this exodus for people I might recognize. They knew I was watching them go and many paused
to turn and look up at me. Few waved. One man, I saw,

picked up a stone and stood as though he were about to throw it at me – I was far beyond his reach – but he was dissuaded from trying by his wife and let the stone drop back to the ground.

Two days ago I had encountered another family making their preparations to go. I had been standing close to the dam when a couple in a nearby cottage started to carry out their possessions. They stacked these on the open ground beside their house, and then, much to my surprise, and before I could intervene, they made a quick blaze of them.

I asked the man why so much was being destroyed, but he refused to answer me, and I saw too late that he had a malformed lip and palate. His wife came out to me and spoke for him. She asked me if I had come to oversee their departure. I denied this, but she did not believe me. She told me they were going to live with her sister six miles away. I congratulated her on having found somewhere so close. A line of spittle ran from the spout of her husband's damaged lip and he wiped this from his chin.

She told me of the village they were going to, but I forget its name, remembering only that it lay over the boundary into the next county and that the woman spoke of it as though it were a thousand miles distant.

Several children came out of the house to assist with the blaze. One, a boy, shared his father's deformity, except the divided lip seemed much worse, revealing more of the child's teeth and gums beneath.

The fire blew its smoke and glowing embers all around us and the ground was blackened by its heat.

There was a rise on the road below me, creating a tendency for the departing families to gather together, and for those without horses to rest there. Ahead, the road levelled and then fell in a long curve, and the individual groups drew apart again. I could not see the first fork in the road which would divide them, nor the further forks and crossroads beyond, where they would be separated and scattered again.

31

I heard, in the usual circuitous way, that there was a fever starting in the valley. My informant was no more specific than that, and by the tone of her voice I understood that this was a commonplace thing. The symptoms she described to me suggested smallpox. Additionally, I read in one of the few week-old newspapers I had managed to acquire that there had been outbreaks of dysentery in some city centres, a rare occurrence that late in the year.

The news served as my excuse for visiting Mary Latimer, whom I had not seen since her own visit a week earlier, and I took with me what few medicines I possessed.

On my way down the valley I came upon a group of men erecting the posts of a sheepfold. I greeted them and they stopped their work. The old stone pen was drowned.

A new one needed building. It was time to gather the sheep. The sheep needed counting. The sheep needed slaughtering. Coils of rusted wire lay alongside them like giant nests.

I climbed the path and went to the house.

I knocked but received no answer. The door was bolted. I walked round the building and peered into it.

A low fire still burned.

Then I climbed to the crest of the rise above the house, hoping for a broader view, and it was upon attaining the top that I saw the two women. They were half a mile distant from me, up-valley, standing together. I started across the slope, calling as I went.

Eventually they heard me and turned. I saw Martha move instantly to stand closer to her sister, and Mary Latimer hold her briefly before leaving her and coming towards me.

'I went to the house,' I said, leaning forward to clear my mouth and to regain my breath. Mary Latimer lifted her apron and wiped my face, as a mother might a child. 'It occurred to me that you'd gone,' I said. I did my best to sound both unconvinced and unconcerned by the notion.

'Without making our farewells?'

'I heard about the fever.'

'Yes, they do like their small dramas.'

'So are you both well?'

'I am. And Martha is fully recovered from her seizure.'

'And otherwise?'

'Otherwise what?'

'I meant how has she been.' My unintentional evasions continued to disappoint her.

'Not well. Restless, sleepless nights. Her attention, her understanding of even the most trivial things is deteriorating. Yesterday she had another fit of screaming which lasted two hours.'

'Caused by what?'

'Who knows. The call of a bird, a creak in the rafters, the sudden understanding of all she has become.'

'What did you do?'

'I left her. I sat with her for an hour and then I came outside. I stayed within earshot of her, and when there was silence I returned. She greeted me as though I had been gone for an instant, as though none of it had happened. She wanted me to sing hymns with her.'

'Hymns?'

'She remembers all the words. It was something else we did together as children. Then afterwards, when our repertoire was exhausted, I did leave her for an instant, to secure the door, and when I returned she shouted at me, accusing me of wanting to abandon her. She spoke as though we had lived together, here, all the time she was absent. She wanted to know where our parents were, where our husbands and all our loving children were.'

'It must have been awful for you,' I said. And again I disappointed her.

'Yes, awful.'

'I brought some medicines. I didn't know what you might have, if there was anything you needed.'

'They say down there that the wind and cold air are cures in themselves.'

'I daresay they have little enough else to put their faith in.'

From where we stood we could see the spreading waters.

'She wanted to come up here and see it.' For the first time since coming to intercept me, Mary Latimer looked back at her sister. The woman waited where she stood, her gaze fixed on the scene below.

'Shall we go to her?'

Mary Latimer shook her head. 'Leave her. I'm afraid you have disappointed her yet again, Mr Weightman.'

'Me? How?'

'Your lake. She expected it to be so much grander.'

'It seems part of my appointed role – to constantly disappoint,' I said.

'And did you once imagine that it might be otherwise?'

'It wasn't something to which I gave much thought.'

'Or at least not until you arrived here among the heathens.'

'No, not until then.'

'I've received word from the asylum,' she said.

'Will you accompany her, or will someone come for—'

'No, I will take her there myself.'

'Is there provision for you to remain with her for a short period, to help her settle there?'

'*She* believes so.' She looked again to the woman.

'But in truth?'

'They do not encourage the relatives or guardians of new committals either to enter with them or to visit them for a given period following their internment.'

'And by not encouraging they mean they forbid.'

'The understanding being, I assume, that because I have absolved myself of all responsibility for her, then I must submit to their every demand, however petty, cruel or unreasonable they might seem to me.'

'And she understands none of this.'

'Do *you* wish to tell her?' She wiped a hand over her face, as though suddenly and fleetingly weary of the great burden placed upon her. 'You mentioned medicines,' she said.

'I doubt there is anything your father would not already have been familiar with thirty years ago.'

She looked into the satchel I held open, but with little enthusiasm.

'Where they lived,' she said, 'my parents, it was a richer place than this. My father would say often enough in his prayers that they were caught up into Paradise and they would never leave it. I envied him his conviction then and I envy him it now.'

I recognized the phrase and sought hard to identify it.

'Saint Paul,' I said eventually.

'In his letter to the Corinthians. I won't flatter you by saying you surprise me. Look over there.' She pointed to a rocky outcrop. 'See? And look beneath us.' Another exposed face rose out of the grass.

'Do they have names?' I asked her.

'Can you not guess? They are known as Saint Peter's Gates.'

'The Gates to Heaven, to Paradise? Here?'

'I imagine that is the interpretation many might give them. It was the name, too, remember, of the gates on Mount Purgatory, guarded by Peter's angels.'

'And is that how *you* choose to see them?'

'My father would have told you that wide is the gate and broad the way that leadeth to destruction. Tell me, will the water rise high enough to cover them?'

'I doubt it, no.'

'So are we even to be denied our own Charybdis and Scylla?'

'I doubt most days you will even have waves.'

'And will it ever freeze completely over? Or would that be too unbearably direct a comparison?'

I did not fully understand the remark. 'In the shallows, perhaps, or during the severest of winters.'

'Then she and I will never see it.'

She looked again to her sister. The woman remained perfectly still, looking down over the valley. Occasionally she raised and then lowered her arm as though pointing something out to an invisible companion. She spoke, too, but her voice was carried away from us in the wind.

'I sometimes think it is the greatest loss of all to bear,' she said. She continued staring at her sister as she spoke. 'To be lost in the truest sense, and yet to remain ever present, to be an ever-present reminder of that loss, the embodiment of loss.'

She paused, perhaps conscious of having told me too much, or perhaps stopped by the sweet taste so suddenly in her mouth.

Afterwards we stood together in the silence of the hills for a long while. And by silence, of course, I mean the countless small sounds other than those of our own voices, of which so-called silence is all too often composed.

Eventually, having insisted upon her accepting my medicines, I told her I would return soon, and that she was to get word to me if her sister's health worsened. She acquiesced to all this in silence.

I raised my hand to Martha, but the woman, despite looking directly at me, gave no indication that I existed.

Later, returning home alongside the dam, I saw the other sufferers there, all of them standing with their faces turned into the wind, and all with their mouths wide open, as though the wind were indeed a proven cure and they were drinking it in.

32

Two days later I was walking on the far slope above the dam when I was alerted by a commotion below me. I heard shouting, and someone ringing a handbell, a sure sign of some alarm or other, calling the faithful to witness or to protest. A small crowd had assembled. A group of men ran across the top of the dam, leaving the sheep they had been penning to wander behind them.

I turned my attention back to the dwellings, where I saw a second group of men marching in procession towards the chapel, women and children running alongside them. Looking more closely, I saw that these men carried hammers and pickaxes, and only then did I realize that the wreckers had returned.

I hurried as best I could down the steep slope.

Arriving at the dam, I composed myself.

Someone at the far side saw me and shouted out, and those below turned to watch me come. I began to regret having been so hasty in my desire to intervene, but I felt justified in my actions by the belief that my sudden appearance might at least bring a brief stay of execution to whatever it was the wreckers were there to destroy, and that an opportunity for negotiation, however illusory, now existed.

The tolling bell fell silent, and I felt as I had felt wading into the whirlpool.

I left the dam and followed the path leading to the chapel. I knew it was unlikely that the building itself was the focus of the wreckers' attention, and supposed that their march on it was all part of their method. I felt encouraged by the realization. I would make it the point of my intercession and divert them from it. The men and women and children parted before me.

I stopped at some distance from the wreckers, and under the pretext of taking off my pack I looked around me at all the other abandoned buildings against which their energies might be more usefully directed now that the water was so high and rising so rapidly.

It occurred to me then that they might have been sent following the departures of several days earlier; their appearance was too much of a coincidence for it to be otherwise. And realizing this, it also struck me that there must either be an informant inside the valley, or someone watching from beyond who was able to inform the Board of these opportunities. If there was some Judas within, then I was at a loss to identify him.

I looked more closely at the local men surrounding the

wreckers. Many stood with lengths of wood or some implement in their hands. Few looked serious about fighting. None of the wreckers seemed in the least concerned about the outcome of the confrontation. Some of them taunted the local men. Others made less vocal suggestions to the women, and tempers rose as I made my final approach. Several of the locals fell in behind me. I wished they had stayed apart.

I came into the space in front of the chapel. I called a greeting to the wreckers, but this was received only with laughter.

One of them stepped forward. 'I'm Tozer,' he said. 'These men are here under my charge on the authority of—'

'The Water Board. I know,' I said, hoping to deflate him. I introduced myself.

'*You're* Weightman?' he said.

I asked him why he found that so strange.

'We thought you were long gone,' he said.

'Gone?'

He was a short, heavily built man, with shoulders that hunched forwards. He held a lump hammer across his chest.

'They told us you might still be here, but they said they couldn't be certain. They thought you might be back in Halifax doing it all from there.'

'They *know* I'm still here,' I said. 'So if you've come to—'

He turned to the others. 'He thinks he knows best which buildings we ought to attend to.' He made sure the watching locals heard this, perhaps hoping to suggest to them that *I* was the informant.

'I make my recommendations based solely on an under-standing of those buildings already long abandoned and those threatened most by the rising water,' I said loudly, but knowing how ineffectual I sounded even before the stilted words were out. I pointed to several half-drowned structures further down the slope. 'Some of which, I imagine, Mr Tozer, are no longer accessible even to you, unless you wish to get your feet wet.'

He turned his back on me and addressed his men. He asked them what they wanted to attack first, and they all cried, 'The chapel,' further convincing me that they had been primed and that this was not their true target.

One of the men ran towards the burial-ground gate and stood as though about to swing at it with his hammer. But he stopped short and his blow found no target. Tozer shouted to him to get back with the others.

I approached closer to him. 'Played your trump card?' I said, quietly enough for him alone to hear.

I turned back to the watchers. 'They have a legitimate task to perform,' I shouted, and then waited for the chorus of disapproval to subside. 'But they have no right, under provision made by the Board, to turn their attention to any dwelling still inhabited or in other use. Those provisions are listed under regulations—' And here I fabricated a list of numbered clauses and sub-clauses with which to stamp my authority even harder on the proceedings. I paused, allowing the weight of my announcement to sink in. I was pleased with myself. I wondered if Tozer would call my bluff, but I saw by the way he looked from one group of men to another that this was unlikely. 'Any contravention of the regulations,' I said, 'will be liable to restitution or compensation by the Board under—' And here I scattered another crop of fictions around me.

Tozer came back to me and pushed his face close to mine. His breath smelled of tobacco.

'They warned me you were a man clothed in writing,' he said.

'Then they were right,' I said.

'But they still think you're back in Halifax, hidden away in some hotel or other and making it all up from there.' He smiled broadly. 'Tell me, why *are* you still here? They can't have expected you to stay this long.'

'My contract stipulates—'

'They hand out their contracts like pennies to beggars.'

'Nevertheless, they have an obligation to—'

'An obligation they forget the minute the ink's dry on your name. That's it as far as they're concerned. They obey the law as they see it. Everyone gets what they want. No one expects you to get too excited about your part in it all.'

'Who told you to come today?' I said, refusing to be drawn so publicly.

He looked slowly around him, pausing at the sight of a number of local men. I followed his gaze, but no one gave themselves away to me. Then he tapped his nose. 'Why would we need someone here to tell us what to do?'

'But there *is* someone,' I said, and knew from his response that I was right.

'Why don't *you* paint a nice big black cross on the doors of all those places more worthless than the rest,' he said. 'Then we'll know where to go.' He came even closer to me. 'But don't worry, Mr Weightman, we'll get to them *all* in time. Every single one of them. Even this ruin of a chapel.

By the time we've finished, you won't have the faintest idea that there was ever anything here.'

I took several paces back from him. 'You will instruct your men to approach no closer than fifty yards to the chapel,' I shouted.

He shook his head at the easy advantage I had taken. Then he raised up his hammer and pushed past me to a nearby sizing shed that had stood empty since my arrival. He called for the others to follow him, which they did, coming now more cautiously through the onlookers.

They set about their work on the building with a vengeance, putting on a show for the watching crowd. Tozer and several others climbed immediately on to the roof and swung their hammers into its slabs, breaking them and letting them fall into the shell beneath. There was no glass remaining in the windows and the frames were smashed in seconds. One man hammered at the chimney stack and then leaned against it until it gave way and collapsed. Few of the men took heed of their own safety amid the destruction.

And after the sizing shed they turned to other structures, splitting into smaller gangs and going in search of separate targets.

Later, I sought out Tozer before returning home. I found him sitting on a balk of timber drinking from an earthenware jar. He shielded his eyes at my approach and looked up at me.

'You must have started from close by to have arrived here so early,' I said.

'Close enough.'

'Is it well-paid work?'

'It's work.'

There were tales of some of the early wreckers having

looted recently abandoned homes in which belongings had been left behind awaiting later retrieval. I guessed that these tales were as untrustworthy as any other.

He handed up the jar to me and I took it.

'Truth is,' he said, 'I'm more surprised to find *them* here than you. They know what's coming, so why do they cling on?' There was no coarseness in his voice or manner now that there was no show to put on.

'Like shipwrecked sailors to wreckage,' I said.

'First time we came, we had instructions to offer the wrecking work to them.'

'To get them on your side?'

'Who cares what side they're on. I don't. Do you?'

I shrugged rather than commit myself to the uncertain truth. I took a drink from the jar and gave it back to him.

'Tell them there will be fewer reports in future,' I said.

'Me? Tell them? I see as much of them as you do. And, like you, I do what they tell me to do. It suits my purpose to do it, and it suits theirs to have it done a long way away from them and out of their sight. We've got a lot more in common, you and me, than you'd ever allow.'

'Perhaps,' I said.

'You'll no doubt want to write something about all this.'

'What would be the point?'

'You could tell them how efficiently the work was carried out, how courteous we were, how little disruption we caused, how vital our task was.'

'I could even pretend to have had some important role in the proceedings myself.'

'Why not?' He held out the jar again. 'I don't know why you stay,' he said. 'Me, I'd have gone mad stuck up here all this time.'

'Perhaps I have,' I said.

'No, you haven't. They wouldn't pay a madman what they pay you. Although I did once hear a tale about a member of the Board who went on being paid a good salary for a year after he'd died.'

33

After an absence of a month, my frog-man ranter returned to visit me. I was approaching my gate after a day's work when I saw him standing there with his lean grey hounds stretched out in the grass around him. He watched me draw near, taking some pleasure, I imagine, in seeing me struggle with my cases up the final slope. Other than pausing to observe him where he stood for several seconds, I chose to ignore him. He, too, seemed unwilling to come any closer or to approach me directly.

I went inside. My hearth was cold and I rekindled a fire there, but one which would burn with little real warmth for some time yet.

He knocked at my door.

'Stay where you are,' I called out to him, hoping to make

my feelings at seeing him again immediately clear to him.

But he pushed the door open and came in anyway. He stood for a moment on the threshold and looked around the room.

'I imagined they might have provided better for you than this,' he said, more amused than surprised by what he saw.

'You and I alike,' I said.

'Chimney needs sweeping.'

'I daresay.'

'Did they truly offer you nowhere better to lodge?'

'So, once again you have come to mock me and to no doubt disclose your own impossible plans for the future,' I said to him. I let my hands fall to the table with a louder bang than was necessary.

'Was I here before?' he said.

The remark made me cautious.

'You came days after my own arrival. You showed me your feet.'

He sat for a moment in wonder, and it occurred to me for an instant that I had mistaken his identity. He looked again around the room.

'Was I in here?' he said.

'No, you did all your ranting then outside.'

'Is that what I was?' He seemed genuinely confused by what I said to him.

I sat opposite him at the table, and the fire slowly took hold between us.

'Do you not remember?' I asked him. 'You showed me the webbing of your toes and told me about your hands.'

He held these up and examined them.

'Did I alarm you?'

'You seemed to alarm yourself more than you alarmed me.'

He laughed at this. 'I'm beginning to remember it, flooder.' He went to the fire and attended to it as though it were his own. He broke the peat into smaller pieces and scattered shavings from the hearth basket amid these. The flames rose fierce and crackling for an instant before dying down.

'Were the dogs with me?' he said.

It was clear to me by then that he truly had no recollection of that earlier visit. His entire manner was changed. The same grey hair covered his face, the same dark eyes lay in their sockets, but everything else about him was different.

'Ought I to make my apologies?' he said.

'No more than a hundred others.'

'So, they welcomed you among them as the saviour you believed yourself to be,' he said. He locked his hands on the table and pointed his forefingers at me.

'Except I never claimed any such thing.' I tried hard to remember what else he might have told me, might have predicted or foreseen.

'Perhaps not, but did no tiny part of you ever believe it?'

'You were fond of all these riddles and sly allusions then, I remember.'

He considered this for several moments.

I felt the first feeble heat from the fire.

'They reckon that at times I am not right in my head.' He looked hard at me and smiled.

'You are certainly a more acceptable proposition in this state than formerly.'

ROBERT EDRIC

His smile became laughter. 'What was I going to do – live in your pond like a merman?'

'Like a giant frog,' I said.

'Ah, yes. I shall, of course, spare both of us that particular embarrassment.'

'Do whatever you please,' I told him.

He considered me closely. 'Surely, that is not disillusion I detect. I seem to remember you all puffed up with the thing.'

'A minute ago you did not even remember having been here.'

'It comes and goes,' he said, winking at me.

I took the kettle and settled it into the rising fire.

Outside, one of his dogs barked and he cocked his head to this. 'His mother died,' he said, and it was several seconds before I realized he was speaking about the barking dog.

'I'm sorry.'

'In Bradford. A man shot her.'

'For what reason?'

'For no reason other than that he was sighting a rabbit along his gun when she chased it and caught it.'

'Was she killed cleanly?'

'Only when I reached her.'

'And the man who shot her?'

'Pointed the same gun at me until I was long out of sight.' He waited for more from the animal, but nothing came. Their lives, it again occurred to me, were no more or less harsh or uncertain than his own.

'Why are you back here?' I said to him.

'I am back because I shall return no more.'

'Then are you here to say farewell to someone?'

He bowed his head.

'Who? Have you seen them?'

'I have.'

'Is it Mary Latimer?' I said, though not knowing why this sudden guess came into my head, but then knowing by his raised face that I was right in my guess.

'And some accuse *me* of having second sight,' he said.

'It was merely a guess.'

'I knew you would have sought her out, or she you.'

A thought occurred to me. 'And you knew she and Martha were watching us from high on the hill on the occasion of your last visit.'

He acknowledged the truth of this with a further nod.

'Had you been to see her then?'

'To see Martha. I know the two of them from all those years ago.'

'Then you knew Martha before—'

'Before she lost her own reason, yes.'

'Then she—'

'What? She must have lost hers before I lost my own?'

'I was going to say that she – Mary – must have been pleased to see you. I know how hard life has been for her since her return, what isolated lives they lead.'

'My apologies. I sat for an afternoon with Martha and she was as clear in speech and reason to me then as I am to you now. I understand all that this implies, of course, but it is how she was with me. Or perhaps you believe the madness in me cancels out her own and we can sit and talk as equals.'

'You speak as though she had some control over how she behaved, over the workings of her mind.'

'No – I speak as someone standing on the edge of that

same abyss. Were I the ranter you believed me to be at our last encounter, I would not be sitting here like this with you now.'

Neither of us spoke for several minutes, both of us watching the fire and the kettle.

'Forgive me,' he said eventually. 'Perhaps I, too, have become over-accustomed to everyone else knowing what is best for me.'

'Meaning?'

'Meaning I am not the lonely, lost or forlorn soul you might imagine me to be.'

'You have a family?'

'All the worthless parts of one. And a home, built on stone and raised to last. Not like this poor place.' He looked again at the damp-pocked walls and then up at the ceiling.

'Then we all misjudge you,' I said.

'No. You see only what you are shown.'

'And is that what you are also telling me in relation to Martha Latimer?'

He shook his head.

'Tell me,' I insisted.

He considered this for several minutes before speaking again, and when he spoke he told me only the barest details of what had happened to him – that a railway company had built a line where he lived, that his home and the surrounding land had been compulsorily purchased – 'stolen' was the word he used – and that he had fought the railway company in the courts for three years before finally being forced to succumb to the weight of their authority, empty promises and wealth.

I guessed, too, that the balance of his mind had also been lost in the fight.

'Three years I stood against them. And on the day I could no longer afford to pursue the matter through the courts, they sent a gang of men to pull off my doors and put stones through every pane of glass in every one of my windows. The same day.'

'But you were compensated, surely?'

'You cannot measure three years of living against three years of dying, Mr Weightman. You might imagine it possible, but it is not.'

'And you see the same thing happening now to Mary and Martha Latimer.'

'To everyone here.'

'I sincerely hope you are wrong in that judgement.'

'Of course you do. Because otherwise how would the scales of your own mind and conscience ever again be balanced equal?'

I could frame no reply to this.

'How long ago did all this happen?' I said eventually.

'Seventeen years,' he said.

'Seventeen years?'

'Yesterday,' he said. 'Yesterday.'

He rose from the table and began fastening up his coat.

'You are welcome to stay,' I told him. My hand was still on the kettle.

He shook his head.

'Shall I mention you to Mary Latimer?'

'To Martha, perhaps.'

'Will you go and see her again?'

He shook his head.

'She'll be sorry to have missed you.'

'I watched her earlier from the hillside above the ruins of their home. She would not have recognized me. The sight of me would have sent her screaming indoors in fright.'

'But Mary would have known you.'

'Oh, she would have known me.'

'But you think she would have kept you from seeing her sister?'

'It was beyond me even to ask her.'

'You being a madman yourself.'

'You see my dilemma.' He extended his hand to me and then went to the door. He opened it and I saw that his dogs were waiting directly outside. One of the animals rubbed its bony head against his knee, and I guessed immediately which of the creatures this was.

'I shall tell them you came,' I called after him.

'I know you will,' he said, and then the door closed behind him.

34

I left my house to be greeted by the urgent rising of a flock of crows (the collective noun, I know, is a 'murder', but that has always struck me as being far too melodramatic) that had congregated in the grass at the front. The birds abound in the district, riding the winds seemingly without concern for where they are blown. There are few perfect specimens; most sport torn tails or missing wing feathers, and some display patches of aberrant white. They flock to the dead sheep on the moors like flies to ordure.

I stood back to let the mass of birds clear the ground, deafened by their clamour. They rose awkwardly, frequently colliding with each other in their struggle to gain height. Some rose only as high as the wall, where they settled and then turned to face me, bucking their heads at me and cawing in anger at being disturbed.

Feathers floated to the ground around me and I gathered these up. It had been an occupation of Helen and Caroline to create pictures and patterns from gathered feathers, though ones more colourful and decorative than the specimens I now collected. The birds on the wall fell silent.

Later that same day I met a man who remarked on the feathers still protruding from my pocket. He told me it was bad luck to carry them. I stopped him from plucking them out, and my reluctance to be rid of them, of the memory they held, offended him. He told me that if the opportunity arose I should observe the birds in coition – those were not his words – because when their congress was at its most urgent both the male and the female birds bled from their eyes. He told me of the birds he had stoned among his lambing sheep whose faces had been red with the blood of their mating, and when I suggested that this might have been more a consequence of their feeding he dismissed the remark with a snarl.

35

'I met an acquaintance of yours,' I said.

She paused briefly in her walk beside me.

'You were visited by him,' she said. Her eyes had been on the ground before she spoke. She kept her head bowed.

'How did you know?'

'What does it matter?'

I stopped walking.

'What, Mr Weightman? Did you imagine that I would *not* know that he had been to see you?'

I resented the challenge in her voice.

'So were you waiting for me to raise the subject of his visit?'

'He comes here every few months. The last time he came he visited Martha and the two of them spent several hours together. He believes that he, too, might have been committed to an asylum. But presumably you know all this already. He will have told you everything.'

'I know he points a finger at you for having committed Martha when she might have lived a life as carefree as the one he now lives.'

She laughed at this. 'Black and white, Mr Weightman, right and wrong. Oh, how you like the lands and seas and islands of your own little globe well ordered and severely locked in their places.'

'Meaning what? All I meant to say was—'

'All you meant to say was that you agreed with him in some measure, this new *friend* of yours.'

'You misjudge me. I see that no other course was open to you.'

'No, but perhaps the smallest of doubts is already forming in your mind: perhaps I could have kept her from all that; perhaps I should have implored harder for my husband to make some better arrangement for her; perhaps I should have denied myself some small part of the comforts and privileges I went on to enjoy while she was all those years locked away.'

She stopped walking and clasped a hand to her mouth. She stood into the wind with her eyes closed.

I regretted all I had brought so suddenly back to the surface, all I had yet again forced her to face in the open when she faced it inwardly every waking moment of her life.

'All I meant by the remark was that I understood what little choice—'

'*Choice*, Mr Weightman? *Choice?* Choice does not apply. There is no choice, there never was any choice. *Choice*, Mr Weightman, is what *you* enjoy, and you alone. Where else does this choice exist? Look around you, as far as you can see, and tell me where.' She opened her eyes and flung her arms around her.

After a minute or so of this rage, she grew calm and let her arms fall.

I could think of nothing to say to her.

Eventually, she came closer to me and said, 'He visits her because he sees himself all too clearly in her. He knew her at the very outset of her illness, when a good deal of her old self still remained. Who knows, perhaps he even harboured some romantic notion towards her. Perhaps he saw what he saw, and seeing how tenuous then was the hold of her illness, he imagined he might yet save her. I wish I could make my own confusion clear for you. Perhaps I wish he *had* been more to Martha. Perhaps then I would not have been so alone with it all. Perhaps every decision made on her behalf would have not been so great a weight on my shoulders alone. Perhaps if her illness had held off only a single year longer she might have been courted and married and then she would have had a husband to make all those impossible decisions, those *choices* of yours. Or perhaps we might extend our imagining even further and see her illness five or ten years away from her, perhaps a doting husband and half a dozen doting daughters of her own to care for her. Imagine my own role in those proceedings then, Mr Weightman. Imagine what luxury of choice *I* might have possessed.'

'It was never my intention to judge you,' I said, knowing how inadequate these words sounded.

'Nor his,' she said.

'Circumstances, I suppose,' I said. 'The parallels between Martha's life and his own.'

'The comparisons are too convenient,' she said. 'I prefer not to make them. Believe me, they are no help.'

'No,' I said.

She rested against a post beside our path.

There was rain in the air.

I had encountered her crossing the high moor and knew immediately from her slow pace and the direction she walked that she was bound for no destination other than the emptiness in which to wander alone with her thoughts.

'When he first came he showed me his toes,' I said, and she laughed at this.

'When we watched you.'

'Before I knew who you were.'

'When you still considered yourself apart from all this.'

'Before my own choices were scattered in the wind.'

She acknowledged this, but said nothing, making it clear to me that she did not entirely concur with what I said.

'He told me then that he would make the reservoir his own watery kingdom and that he would live upon the fishes within it.'

I expected she might laugh again, but instead she said, 'He is a truthful man. We must never doubt for an instant that whatever he says he does not mean.'

Now it was my turn to acknowledge this gentle reproach.

'One of his dogs was killed,' I said.

She considered this. 'Then he will have been mortally wounded himself. He believes his family no longer cares for him. It is why he leaves them to wander with his animals. The first thing they do upon his return is put him in a bath and scrub him clean. What is it, do you imagine, that they believe they are washing away?'

'He never even told me his name,' I said.

'His name is Jacob Wright,' she said. 'See how much more of an ordinary man it makes him.'

'He told me something of the cause of his wandering.'

'It was no cause, merely something for him to blame.'

'Oh?'

'His wife and family were never reluctant to leave their home. It was poorly located and built in an unsanitary place. Three babies his wife lost. Why should *that* not have played a greater part in his sense of loss and growing madness?'

'Perhaps he distinguishes between those acts of God and the acts of men.'

'More choice. A whole ripe tree of choice from which to pluck.'

'Jacob Wright,' I said, seeing how much better clothed he was with the name than without it.

'He was an engineer, like yourself,' she said.

It was an almost intolerable thought.

'What will become of him?'

'Who knows? Is a man mad simply because another man points a finger at him and calls him mad?'

'Then I wish he might be left in peace,' I said.

'In this day and age? The nets are cast, Mr Weightman.'

I said nothing in reply.

She came to me and touched me briefly, as though to remove any pain she might have caused me by her earlier attack.

'I wish I'd known his name and history from the beginning,' I said.

She nodded. 'Perhaps there are people here who might think the same of you.'

'To know about me?'

'To understand something that might make their plight a little easier to bear.'

Their plight?

'They have only to ask,' I said.

'They would no sooner ask than reveal their own webbed feet to you.' She turned her face to the sky above us. The wind drew out her unbound hair. 'I ought to be getting back and you ought to be getting on with your work.'

I waited until she lowered her face, and then said, 'How many of those dutiful daughters would Martha have had?'

'Three,' she said immediately. 'Abigail, Rebecca and Mary.'

'And her husband?'

'A country doctor who loved her and cared for her, and who kept her comfortable and safe inside a well-appointed house inside a high-walled garden within a community of people who knew her and cared for her also.' She tried not to smile at all I had so easily exposed.

'And grandchildren?' I said.

'I try hard not to think of them,' she said. 'There are limits to my indulgence; I know what purpose it serves.'

'And you never confuse this imagining with choice.'

'Never. But I shall not persevere in trying to persuade *you* of that.'

I let her know that I believed her. These beliefs were the props which kept her upright, just as the wind appeared to do on occasion, and she tested her beliefs as she leaned into the wind and tested that, too. I saw that she was strength and reason and belief enough for the pair of them.

We parted and I watched her go. She was quickly lost to

my sight, and only when she was finally gone did I thank her for not having asked me the names of my own unborn, beautiful and doting children.

36

In my dream I am walking across a field, the saturated surface of which is repeatedly rent open beneath me, causing me to leap from one spot to another, uncertain if the ground where I aim to land is solid or liquid or somewhere in between. It is a recurrent act – if such a thing can be said of the sleeping mind – only this time varied by the presence of a great crowd of people standing around me on the solid ground there, every one of them applauding my expertise at avoiding the pitfalls and soakings, and all of them shouting for me to run to them, these men, women and children all with their arms outstretched towards me, each one of them urging me to save myself. It is too large a crowd to be composed solely of the local inhabitants, and I recognize faces from long ago and hear voices I had never thought to hear again, but these come only in snatches of unintelligible language, quickly lost to me amid the overall excitement.

I cannot say for certain that I hear in my dream the hatred, mockery and contempt that I know must season the calls of many in the crowd, but I hear something in that surge of yelling which, like the cry of a child, can be neither disguised nor ignored.

In places I sink to my waist; elsewhere the ground rises beneath me so that I stand clear of the water. At times I am wearing my high boots, and my leaping from place to place in the shallows is no more than a game, another act put on by me to entertain my watchers. And at other times my feet and legs are bare and I jump into submerged pools and land up to my waist in the coldest water. I feel my feet sucked into the mire beneath me. Several men throw ropes to me, but these fall short of where I stand, and the ones that do come close, the ones for which I might reach out, are quickly snatched away as my hand approaches them. When this happens, the laughter and the shouting is at its loudest, and it occurs to me then to stop jumping, to land upon some more solid ground and to stand there motionless, thus depriving my audience of its entertainment. But when I attempt to do this, and by my stillness and silence remove myself from this dreamed suffering, the solid ground upon which I stand turns to liquid, and I know – even in my sleep I know – that there is no end to my ordeal except waking into darkness.

37

'Do you never speak of her?'

Mary Latimer paused briefly to await my reply.

I had mentioned Helen and my distant, former life – the life from which I now felt myself so far detached that it might have been the life and history of another man completely.

'She died and it seemed to me as though I had lost everything I ever possessed to lose,' I said. 'We had planned too far and too well into the future. When she died, I felt as though I had been deceived in some way.'

'I won't make you smile by saying I know exactly what you mean.'

'You would know better than most,' I told her. I signalled to her that I appreciated the kindness intended in her remark.

Martha walked ahead of us. I had encountered the pair

of them on the far side of the dam. I was surprised to see them so close to the dwellings and told her so.

'She insisted on coming,' she said. 'It was another of the places we used to walk. We avoided the houses by crossing the river downstream. We kept ourselves to this side.'

'Was it where you came as girls?'

'It was.'

She watched her sister for a moment.

Martha picked at the branches of a bush, collecting what few dead leaves it still held.

'She thinks we are out gathering berries,' she said. 'It was what we did. I used to object to being sent on the task, but she always derived a great deal of pleasure from it.'

Martha turned and waved to us and we both waved back. She held up what she had so far gathered. Most of the leaves fell from her hand, but she seemed not to notice this.

'Was it a short illness?' she said.

'Short and sudden and thorough. Though when its first signs showed and the doctors were sent for, I was convinced it was nothing – an autumn cold – and that, young and otherwise healthy as she was, she would quickly recover from it. Caroline and I sat with her as she rested and spoke with her about all our arrangements. The wedding was then only months away. There was no possibility – no possibility whatsoever – that her full recovery was not guaranteed and that it would not be swift and complete. What was this one small thing against all our hopes and preparations?'

'But instead it took hold of her, ravaged her and killed her.'

I knew there was no callousness intended by the remark.

'It took hold of us both,' I said. 'Ravaged us both.'

'Were you with her at the end?'

'After a fortnight of tremors and sweating, of heat and cold and cramps, she grew calm and her breathing at last seemed easy. The doctor who had attended her latterly expressed his relieved and considered opinion that the worst was finally over and that we might now expect a full recovery. And because I believed him, because I could believe nothing else, I wept in my relief. Both Caroline and I – we held each other and we wept. We even performed a little celebratory dance in the corridor outside the bedroom. Her parents were beneath us and I heard the man repeat the same words to them. I heard their own exclamations and prayers. I held Caroline as tightly as I had ever held her. She was Helen, see? In that instant she was her healthy and recovered sister, and we both understood that. I clung to her and she clung to me. My tears ran down her neck and hers down mine. I have never experienced a joy such as I experienced then, never before, and certainly never since.'

'A joy that made what was to follow all the more painful for you.'

I could only nod.

'How soon afterwards did she die?'

'The same night. We had a day, twelve hours of being buoyed upon our raft of hope and celebration. We prayed, we gave thanks, we redoubled our efforts to talk at every opportunity of the coming wedding.'

'She was recovered enough to do this?'

'Not Helen. I meant Caroline and I.'

'I see.' She remained close to me, her eyes passing from me to her sister and then back to me.

'I remember that she and I went for a walk,' I said. 'It seemed we had been cooped up in that house for a month.

It was a fine day. We walked to the boathouse and sat there looking out over the water. She held my hand. We told each other that our prayers had been answered and that the path of our three lives together – for she intended staying close to us when Helen and I were wed – was again straight and clear ahead of us. I sometimes sensed that Helen was envious of the easy understanding between her sister and myself. She and I possessed a similar understanding, of course, but the tie between Caroline and myself was in some small and vital way different. She was always more direct with me than Helen was. I suppose many might consider her less feminine. She called her sister a "flutterer-of-eyelashes" and herself a "pointer-of-fingers".'
This sudden memory of the words and of her voice when she said them caused me to feel suddenly chilled. 'She told me often enough that Helen and I were not well suited to each other, but it was only her way of avoiding saying a great deal more, and she never once doubted that her sister and I would make each other happy. I remember I once asked her what kind of man she herself hoped to marry and she refused to speculate. She said she would not blinker herself on the subject, and that she would only know what kind of man when he arrived. It would have pleased me no end to have heard her say that she would marry a man like me, and she sensed this and swore vehemently that she would never marry a pond-builder or a pipe-layer. A beggar-poet would suit her better, she said.'

Mary Latimer smiled at this. 'Then she saw neither the poet nor the beggar in you, Mr Weightman.'

'I was never either. Besides, for what would I ever truly have the need to beg?'

She avoided answering me by looking back to her sister and calling her name. Again, Martha responded with a wave.

'That poor bush will consider itself harshly treated if she does not soon move on to another,' she said.

'Perhaps no other possesses such ripe berries,' I said.

The slope beneath us cut off all view of the dam and the water, and to stand there and look up the valley as we were able to, you might imagine that neither the wall nor the reservoir yet existed. I pointed this out to her and she agreed, adding that this was why she had brought Martha there.

'There are still some things I am able to do for her,' she said. 'Little enough, but they mean a great deal to her.'

'Do you believe she sometimes imagines herself to be a child again on these errands?'

'It would be something to hope,' she said.

'So – shall I one day become a beggar, do you think?' I asked her.

'We are none of us above it,' she said.

'I begged for Helen to be spared,' I said. 'I begged for her life, for her health and her strength to return. What good then was my begging?'

'And how soon did you know that all this talk of recovery was a false dawn?'

'Soon enough. Her fever returned. She fitted and vomited continuously until another of the doctors was able to return and sedate her. He seemed surprised at the other man's prognosis.'

'And in that moment you felt the world pulled from under you.'

'Felt it pulled away and felt myself pushed into the emptiness it left behind.'

'And she died soon after.'

'An hour after the man had gone. His sedatives stopped her fitting. She still vomited a little, and Caroline and I took it in turns to hold her head so that she would not choke. Her mother and father slept in the adjoining room and were in and out at the slightest sound. I see now what little account I took of their own anguish.'

'Did she die in your arms?'

'Caroline and I held her head between us. A particularly violent bout of retching occurred, made all the worse by her remaining barely conscious throughout, unable to hold up her own head or to support herself in the bed. We fetched bowls and cloths and warm water between us.'

'You need tell me no more,' she said, though the offer was made for my sake alone.

But I could not stop myself. I could not stop myself from saying the words, *And then she died.*

In the midst of a violent spasm she blew out her cheeks, opened wide her mouth, let her eyes roll to look directly up at me, and died. Caroline cradled her sister's head all the tighter and started to keen, and this unbearable noise summoned her parents and they too were with their daughter within seconds of her death, her father on his knees beside the bed, her mother holding so tightly to the grieving, living daughter that you might imagine she too was in danger of being taken from them.

It lasted like that for an hour, before Caroline finally fell silent and we were able to disengage ourselves, one from the other, until only the bed and its corpse remained unmoving, and those of us who raised ourselves from the body wandered like ghosts around the dimly lit room in an emptiness so dark and so cold and uncertain that none of us knew any longer what we did or thought.

I paused in all this remembering to take account of the tears in my eyes, which ran into the corners of my mouth.

'And then she died,' I said, not knowing whether I was repeating myself or saying the words for the first time.

Mary Latimer took out a handkerchief and wiped my face.

'And you have been alone ever since,' she said.

I closed my eyes.

She wiped my chin and then traced the tips of her fingers along my jaw to see what remained.

When I opened my eyes she was looking at me intently.

'Perhaps I'll ask Martha to turn her leaves into jam for you,' she said.

I could not help but laugh at the remark.

She returned her handkerchief to her sleeve, where she must have felt the wetness of my tears against her arm.

38 _____

This morning I descended the slope to discover the corpses of four supposedly drowned sheep laid out across the path, their fleeces flattened and matted by the rain which had been falling all night. They were thin beasts, with black faces. It is two days since I was last on the path and they were not there then. Their appearance is a puzzle to me. Not because I do not understand what they are intended to represent – the message they send to me – but because I am uncertain as to the intention behind the act. Am I to be provoked this late into some response? Is there someone above all others in the valley whose resentment will not abate?

Further along I encountered a group of men gathering stones in a field. It was clear to me by their response to my greeting that they knew of the corpses and might have had some hand in putting them there.

The result of their labour lay in a small mound beside them, and having paused briefly to acknowledge me, the men returned to their work, searching out and retrieving the stones as though they were a valuable crop. To have asked them why they did this with the water only six feet below them, and soon to cover the field in which they stood, would have served no purpose. The condemnation of futility carries no strength here.

Considering the dead sheep, I was later reminded of a flood I had witnessed four years earlier in the Vale of Evesham. A small dam there had been poorly constructed and had begun to fracture from the day the full weight of the water was accumulated behind it. A warning to evacuate those close downriver was issued, but largely ignored. Engineers advised that the sluices be opened to reduce the pressure, but the owner of the reservoir dismissed all this as scaremongering.

The dam broke in the night and the reservoir emptied.

The following morning I watched from a hillside as the body of water rushed below me. It was an area of poultry breeding, and my strongest memory of the small flood was of seeing thousands of drowned white hens go floating rapidly past me in the current, looking from that height like nothing more than the windblown scattering of apple blossom in a May shower.

39 _____

Mary Latimer came to me across the dam. She stood beside me and looked out over the water. I waited for her to speak.

'A child died,' she said.

'Where?'

She motioned to a house in the shadow of the dam.

This was the first winter the structure had been fully in place, and because of the falling trajectory of the sun, I saw that some houses, including the one below, were now cast into perpetual gloom by it.

'They say their springs are polluted and that drains and cesspools are backed up and overflowing.'

'This is clean water.' I indicated the surface stretching away from us.

'It isn't the first death.'

'Oh?'

'An old woman, already ailing from a great deal else.'

'And are more anticipated?'

'What will you do? Put it in one of your reports? Visit the grieving parents with your condolences?'

Her hostility, accustomed though I had become to it, and knowing what purpose it served, nevertheless continued to unsettle me.

'Is Martha well?' I said, knowing that we were already on the path back to her sister.

'I came away to clear my head.'

'Is she no better?'

'She condemns me. All last night she raged at me for having deceived and betrayed her.'

'In what way, betrayed her?'

'She left that to my own imagination.'

I saw by the darkness around her eyes that she had spent a sleepless night.

'She is now convinced the water has come naturally and that it is a judgement upon us, upon me. I know how laughably predictable the remark might seem, but *she* now chooses to believe it.'

'I don't know what more you can do for her.'

'No,' she said.

'Several days ago a man cursing me for the loss of his home told me it would have been better if their flood – that was what he too called it – had come upon them without warning, in the night as they slept, and that it had swept everything before it in an instant, sparing nothing and no one, no building, no animal, no person. Then, he said, at least everyone would have *pitied* them.'

'They pity themselves enough without any addition.

Life here may be hard, but what do you see any of them doing to make it even the smallest part easier for themselves? They live now as they lived when I determined to leave it all behind me and never to return.'

'He said I was an excuse of a man put in charge of other men's excuses, one after another, and that I smoothed out all the problems for the money-makers at the cost of everyone here.'

'Do you want me to tell you that he was wrong, that again you are misunderstood?'

I leaned over the rim of the dam and looked down at its wall. She moved closer to me.

'I bound her to a chair,' she said. She too looked down at the barely perceptible curve, at the gentle lash of the waves below us.

'Bound her?'

'She would have done herself harm. She tore her clothes. She burned her hand in the fire and I deliberately bandaged it into a ball to soften her blows against herself.'

'Is she alone now?'

'No, someone is sitting with her. She finally fell asleep. I didn't even need to explain why I had secured her. Pity, you see. For me, for her, a surfeit of the ooze.'

'When will she go?'

'Four days.'

Her answer surprised me. I had asked merely to return to the practicalities of the situation.

'So soon?'

'I came down for my mail,' she said. 'There was only this.' She showed me the final eviction notice sent to her by the Board. Its date was the last day of the year, thirty days hence.

'Will you be ready?'

'How long does it take to walk through a door and utter a prayer for the stones behind you to fall in a heap?'

Beneath us, the door of the house where the child had died opened and a man and a woman came out into the half-light. I instinctively withdrew from the rim so they would not see me, but she remained where she stood, watching them closely. I heard the woman's cries, amplified by the structure against which they were cast.

'Can you not bear to watch them?' she said, eventually withdrawing so that she too might not be seen by the grieving couple.

She left me after that, leaving me alone on the structure.

The same man who had long ago told me about the lake at Hangzhou had also repeated a proverb which said that if a man sat for long enough on the bank of a river he would, in time, see the corpses of all his enemies go floating past him. I looked out over the rising lake and thought of those lost archers standing before their crushing wave.

I returned home, encountering no one.

Slender black clouds formed and trailed like ribbons over the far rim of the valley.

I was by then far behind in my report-writing. I had neglected to make several recent surveys, and a great deal else needed to be done. Increasingly, the weather was against me, but this, I knew, was an excuse. I was rising later than usual, and I frequently stayed up into the early hours of the morning and slept until noon. Where previously I had gone out in the sharpest of winds, I now avoided all discomfort.

For all the world knew or cared I might have been a lone envoy sitting at a river station deep inside some unexplored country. Perhaps if I had been, then my growing discontent and uncertainty would have been easier to bear. What excuse was there for it here?

That night I woke, climbed from my bed, knelt beside it and said a brief, late prayer for the suffering woman and the dead child. It was my first prayer in over a year, and was said as much for my own sake as for theirs.

Part Three

40

I know it is a common thing among the poets to talk of the mournful cries of the curlews over these empty places, but the fact remains that their calling – the birds themselves all too often invisible – is so unavoidable and distinct that it cannot easily be dismissed. Too often, above the noise of the wind, it is the only thing to be heard here, and in most instances the cry of the birds is so carried by the wind and distorted by it as to create an unsettling effect in the mind of the solitary listener.

It is now more than fifteen months since I last heard the dawn calls of the peahens on the lawns of Helen's home. I was reminded then, I recall, woken so suddenly in the barely risen sun, of the poem which likened the call of the birds to cries of lost souls wandering in Purgatory.

It seemed all sun and brightening dawns in those days. Here it is all growing darkness and ever-shortening days.

I am told that the springs here are harder to bear by those unaccustomed to them than the autumns, and that the summers – short enough though they are – are longer in coming than they are in passing.

I am frequently warned to make provision for fuel and food in the event of snow. When it comes here it arrives with a suddenness and a ferocity seldom seen further south. Its earliest falls are predicted daily. In the past, men who have been away from their homes here have been kept out of the valley for days and even weeks on end because no progress could be made against the falling and drifting. I am told that a fall of only a few inches under calm conditions might easily be drifted here to six or seven feet in the strong winds.

Several days ago there were reports of falls to the west, and only yesterday word of a fall some miles to the north. The configuration of the higher land in both these directions means that they often receive the first of the winter, and the season is spoken of as though it comes at these outlying places like an unstoppable army, which, having conquered these first defences, is then free to advance further, arriving here with nothing to counter it.

Speculation increases with each passing day of darkening cloud.

From the ridge above my house I can see the distant whitening of the high peaks, and there are days now when the whole dome of sky is so uniformly dark and impenetrable, and without even variation in the shape or shade of cloud, that those days must be considered as little more than lesser nights.

To add to this effect, there are also days, clear days, when the moon is both magnified and clearly visible from dawn to dusk as it curves across the heavens.

I remember the summer's evening ball in Shropshire to celebrate our engagement, planned to coincide with the full moon so that there might be light on the driveway for the coming and going of the carriages.

41

Four days passed since my meeting with Mary Latimer on the dam. I rose early with the intention of visiting her and Martha before her sister's departure. Mary Latimer, I knew, would return later in the day, but I wanted to see them while they were still together and to offer them what little assistance she was still able to decline.

I went by way of the dam, guessing that they would come down from their home to await there the carriage Mary Latimer had hired. I knew she would make arrangements to go early, before there were others around to witness what was happening, and so that she herself might return before dark.

I arrived within sight of the dam and the dwellings and saw no one there. Convinced I was in good time, I waited.

It was there, less than an hour later, that I saw the man to whom I had entrusted my mails. My first thought was to hide myself from him. My letters and packages, few enough to begin with, now scarcely repaid the effort to bring them, and each time I encountered him he behaved towards me as though we had agreed a contract on which I had now reneged. But even as I considered concealing myself, I heard him call my name. I raised my cane to him, and in reply he waved something in the air. I had never before seen him run.

He came to me, an envelope clasped to his chest. There was always some drama attached to these arrivals, always some small ceremony to be endured. I feigned in-difference. I saw my name on the label, saw too that, as previously, my address was written as nothing more than the name of the valley. Another man might have appreci-ated the status this conferred, but I personally regretted that throughout the time I had been there no one had thought to seek out the name of my lodgings from my own mails.

The letter had come only an hour ago. It was fortunate that my carrier had been waiting in expectation of some-thing else when it had arrived. I was a lucky man that he had no other pressing business that day. Had I seen him running? He had run all the way from the mail coach. It had been his intention to run to my home. All his other business would be suspended until my mail was delivered. I manoeuvred myself through this predictable charade, enduring and, where possible, shortening it until I was finally given the letter.

He pointed out to me the word 'Urgent' written in capitals across the top of the envelope. I had already seen this, hoping to keep it out of our negotiations. He urged me to open the envelope, but I told him I was on my way home and that it could wait until I arrived there. Throughout all this I continued to watch for the arrival of Mary Latimer and her sister. I did not want the man to be there when they came.

I waited for them for a further hour, regretting with every cold passing minute that I had not enquired further of their arrangements beforehand.

By mid morning I waited with a growing sense of unease, knowing only that it was beyond me to approach the house and perhaps witness there the last of their awful preparations.

I was about to leave when a woman, older than either Mary Latimer or her sister, approached me. She told me she had been watching me for some time. I explained about the important communication I had come to collect. She then said that she knew the sisters, that she had known them since they were girls, and that she was still occasionally employed by Mary to sit with her sister. She said she had seen me on my first visit to the house. I remembered the figure in the doorway.

'You came in the hope of seeing them,' she said.

I apologized to her for my lie concerning the mail.

'She told you she was taking Martha to the asylum today?'

'She said—'

'They went yesterday. Mary returned late last night.'

'Is she at home now?'

'It would be unwise to intrude,' she said.

Is that what I would be, what I had become to her – an intruder?

'Of course,' I said.

'She was in great distress upon her return.'

'Did you see her?'

'She came to my house to let me know that everything was done and that she was safely back.'

'Then were you privy to all her arrangements?'

'I was there when Martha was born. If Mary deceived you, then it was done for a reason.'

We were approached and passed by several others, some of whom held cloths pressed to their mouths.

The woman had nothing more to tell me. Perhaps she had even been told by Mary Latimer to look out for me and to disabuse me of any misplaced notion of participation in the proceedings I might still have harboured. She left me.

Arriving home, I remembered my letter and went immediately to my desk and slit open the envelope. There was a single sheet inside, upon which I was perfunctorily informed that a delegation of the members of the Board – names and exact numbers as yet unknown – would be paying me a visit to see for themselves the advancements already made and undertaken. I would be required to present myself to these members, to guide them to whatever they might wish to see, and to prepare answers and explanations for any questions they might have for me.

The letter was signed by a clerk on behalf of the Chairman. The date mentioned for the visit was only six days away.

I spent the remainder of the day examining my files. I prepared one itinerary, then another. There was nowhere for the delegation to eat or drink, nowhere for them to rest. What if the weather were bad? How would they come and depart? There was no time to communicate these concerns to the Board. I was alone in my preparations, and all

197

thoughts of Mary Latimer and her sister and what had taken place earlier in the day were cast from my mind.

Later in the evening I remembered that the annual shareholders' meeting was to be held on the twenty-first of December, only ten days after the proposed visit, so perhaps its purpose was nothing more than an opportunity for those members sufficiently interested in the scheme to examine it for themselves prior to reporting their observations to the others.

I had hoped to be reassured by these and countless other explanations, but was not.

My night was sleepless, and by two in the morning I had again had recourse to my medicine. At least afterwards I was able to empty my mind in expectation of the pleasant thoughts and dreams which might flow in to fill it, but which, in truth, have lately seldom come, leaving me adrift in a stupefied miasma of expectation and evasion, the very dusks and dawns now of my existence here.

42

I continued with this preparatory work the following day, too occupied by it to even leave the house. I did occasionally think of Mary Latimer alone in her home, perhaps making the further arrangements necessary for her own departure, or perhaps too sunk in and numbed by her grief for even that; but other than these momentary diversions, I gave her no thought. In truth, I would have to confess that a small part of me had hardened towards her, that I felt my sympathy and concern for her and her sister had in some inexplicable way been abused by her.

I made a plan of work for myself and wrote this down in a series of lists which I pinned to the wall above my desk. When each task was completed I drew a satisfying line of ink through the instruction.

I worked late into the night and fell asleep where I sat.

It was late the next morning when I woke, gratified by the realization that everything was done.

A storm had come and gone in the night, but by noon the rain had stopped, and I walked out to hear it coursing down the hillside all around me. Once-invisible streams on the far side of the valley were now white in their spate and raced in straight, unstoppable lines to the water below.

43

Ensuring that I had not too easily persuaded myself, and that all my preparations were truly completed – that I had not confused effort with achievement or panic with enthusiasm – I went to see Mary Latimer, confident by then of my pathless route over the hill.

I met her where I had first seen her, at some distance from her home.

'I was coming to see you,' she said. Her voice was flat, and she made no effort to convince me of her intentions. I noticed that her hair, which had previously been so carefully kept in place, was unbrushed.

'You feel deceived by me,' she said. 'It's only natural.'

I resisted the urge to tell her to stop telling me how I felt, but saw that in this her understanding and her honesty still outweighed my own.

'It is no consolation,' she went on, 'but you are not alone. What would my father say if he could see what I have done? I betrayed her.'

'Was it an awful parting?'

'I thought they might soften, that I might be allowed in with her.'

'And instead you were turned away.'

'She was taken from me in a small antechamber, a room designed for that specific purpose, no window, no view of the world so suddenly left behind, and a door at either end, the first opened only from the inside, the second from the room beyond.'

'Did you explain the circumstances?'

'What circumstances? I had only moments before she was pulled from me. The second door was already open and with someone waiting beside it. I told her I loved her and that I would see her soon.'

'Did she hear you? Did she understand what was happening to her?'

'I don't know. She only began screaming to be brought back to me once the second door was closed behind her. It was a heavy door, her screams were not so loud; I did not throw myself against it and shout for her to be brought back to me, that a terrible mistake had been made. They left me there alone for several minutes afterwards, time enough, presumably, to compose myself and for someone to return and unlock the outer door.'

What other course of action was open to you? You had no choice.

There was not one of my arguments that would have

persuaded her, not one of them that had not already closed around her heart like a fist.

'When will you see her?' I said.

'I was given a pamphlet. Eight weeks.'

It was a time far beyond all reckoning.

I told her about the visit of the Board, but little of what I said pierced the shell of her own thoughts. The wind at that height pulled at her clothes and she seemed barely to possess the strength or the will to stand into it and remain upright. I held her, but she flinched at my touch and pulled free of me.

'I would rather you occupied yourself with your work ahead and not attempt to visit me,' she said.

'Surely I—'

'We were wrong, you and I, Mr Weightman.'

'About what?'

'About the notion of contagion.'

I knew she was not speaking merely of the contagion of insanity, and had she been in any stronger state I would have disputed what she said.

It resumed raining and she folded her arms around herself.

I left her where she stood. In all the time I had known her, she had at best been only half living through her days there; it was a kind of endurance I understood only too well. And she walked now constantly in the cold wake of her sister's madness, tormented by her loss, and shackled by her grief and by the growing sense of unassailable shame she now felt.

44

I lived myself in what I can only describe as a confused state between this encounter and the arrival of the men of the Board.

The weather continued to worsen – snow fell at the valley head, and the rain and sleet did their customary work elsewhere, confining me to my lodgings.

I slept little and ate only when I was hungry, having no appetite otherwise.

I took a small fever – not a serious illness, and any slight nocturnal delirium I might have suffered was cloaked in the urgency and disarray of my otherwise waking life.

I spent several hours making the room in which I worked presentable. I was still not convinced anyone would want to come this far up the valley, but I felt easier in my mind for having prepared for the eventuality.

I packed those journals and charts I was happy to have inspected, ready to take them to the delegation. I calculated the times of the trains to the closest station, plotted their onward route. I worked out a path across the dam and along the new shore. I knew where the views were most impressive, where the body of water stood at its deepest and broadest. I knew where the sun shone best upon its surface.

I was gratified by the certain knowledge that all my errors of judgement and omission were long since drowned and forgotten. Gratified, too, by the growing realization that, despite my own recent reservations, with this first coming of the men of the Board since my arrival, my role in their work, and in the proceedings of the place itself, could no longer be denied, and might be better understood and appreciated by those on both sides who were now depend-ent upon me. I may have owned neither the land nor the water, but I still possessed these potent and undeniable rights over both.

45

I went again to visit Mary Latimer. I knew that she would not welcome my intrusion, that in all likelihood I would again be condemned by her. Or perhaps I believed that her anger and self-loathing might have subsided in the days since I last saw her, that the jagged edges of her grief might have grown blunt, and that she might now better understand my own part in what had happened.

It was nothing so grand as forgiveness that I sought, merely the opportunity to redeem myself in some small way in her eyes, so that when we eventually did part, we might do so without the seeds of suspicion and mistrust planted quite so deep within us.

I spoke aloud to myself as I went, certain of not being

seen or overheard, practising what I would say to her and replying confidently to all her evasions and rebuffs.

By the time her house was within sight I was convinced that there was nothing she might now say to me for which I had not prepared an answer, nothing she might do or confess that would surprise me and cause in me again the feeling of constantly running behind her, which I had all too often felt during our recent encounters.

I saw from a distance that no smoke rose from her chimney.

Coming closer I saw that the front door was thrown wide open.

I quickened my pace. Snow which had fallen in the night lay moulded and grey in the sunless crevices of the hills beyond.

And then I saw her come round the side of the house, but even as I raised my hand and called out to her, I saw that it was not she, and then quickly identified the old woman who had approached me by the dam.

She heard me calling and waited for me to go down to her. Her anxiety was apparent to me long before I reached her.

'She's gone,' she said.

'Left?'

'Gone.' She grabbed my sleeve and led me into the house. Nothing had changed since my last visit there. Clothes and books and other personal belongings still lay where they had lain then.

'See,' I said. 'She merely went out.'

'The door was open.'

'She didn't secure it properly. Her mind was on her sister. The wind blew it open.' But I knew as I spoke that she was

right and that the place had been abandoned. I saw what
the wind had done to the room.

'Nothing has been taken,' she said. 'A man was up here
yesterday, mid-afternoon. He told me in passing that the
fire was already out and the door blowing open. I would
have come then, only it was soon dark and the snow had
started.'

I went to the hearth and put my hand into the ashes.
They were cold, and damp where rain had come down the
chimney. Rising, I found myself again looking into
the faces of her parents, and I knew in that instant that
everything the woman was suggesting was true.

'She would never have left that,' she said, looking over
my shoulder. 'It was all she had of them.'

'We ought to start searching for her,' I said.

'Search? You and I?'

'Everyone. Anyone.'

'Who is there?'

'Everyone who remains.'

'I meant who is there who cares for her? Few of them
knew her.'

'But surely they won't refuse to—'

'She endeared herself to no one here.'

'And that will stop them from looking in the name of
common humanity?'

She turned away from me rather than confront me with
the truth.

I asked her if she would remain in the house while I
went in search of assistance, but she said she would not.
She came out with me and waited while I secured the door.
Without her knowledge, I had taken the small portrait from
the mantel and it was now in my pocket.

I went down the slope ahead of her; she was infirm and moved slowly.

Reaching the houses, I knocked on doors and explained to everyone who would listen to me what had happened. I told them how long Mary Latimer had been gone, what she had recently endured, how distraught and unsettled she had become. And almost everyone to whom I spoke listened to what I said and either shrugged dispassionately, saying there was nothing to be done, or, at best, tried to convince me that I was wrong and that the drama of the situation was all of my own making. Some even laughed in my face, said that she was nothing to them, that I was even less, and then slammed their doors on me.

I did eventually gather a party of three men who agreed to make a search of the nearby buildings, occupied and empty, and then to follow the edge of the water for as long as the daylight remained. I tried to encourage them to go higher, on to the open slopes, to the places where I considered her most likely to have gone, but they quickly made it clear to me that what little help they were prepared to offer was beyond any negotiation.

We searched and asked for any sighting of her, but to no avail. Someone living below the dam might have seen her walking downriver on the far bank. Someone else said they had seen a woman resembling her two days previously, but at a great distance and at the head of the valley.

I returned eventually to the dam and met one of the searchers there. The others had already returned to their homes. I asked him what time we might resume in the morning, but he told me he would be busy with preparations for his departure. I thanked him for what he had done. On impulse, I gave him what little money I had with me, and only upon receiving this unexpected payment did he offer to encourage others to resume looking.

I left him, little reassured by his words.

46

The next day I searched alone, avoiding the houses and the dam and looking instead towards the valley head, seeing all around me the great expanse of rough ground in which a body might lie hidden for weeks, longer were it soon to be covered by snow.

I quickly saw how little I would achieve by this, and so against my better judgement I returned to the dam.

There were men there who told me they had been searching – they pointed out to me where they had looked – but who did not convince me. They had learned of my payment and wanted the same for themselves. Their lies added confusion to the situation.

I left them and went to the quarry, where she and I had once met, but that too was empty, and the echo of my pointless calls came back to prod me before my mouth was even closed.

I returned home, and for long afterwards I speculated on where she might have gone and what she might have done, and how long and terrible her solitary deliberations might have been.

Stronger winds than usual disturbed my fire and my candles, and smoke filled the room, thickened in the liquid yellow light until it resembled sediment floating in water, and by half closing my eyes and watching its shimmering patterns above and around me I could easily imagine myself dwelling underwater.

I fear now that everyone here is wandering aimlessly in the endless puzzle of a cold and disappointing dream, and that all the certainties and comforts of life have been finally stripped away from them, leaving them lost and direction-less, and with the rudiments of existence itself exposed and unbearably raw.

47

On the morning of the visit I woke early, well before the
risen sun, and completed my preparations. I shaved and
washed and trimmed my hair. I wore my cleanest clothes. I
even took with me a clean pair of boots to change into upon
reaching the dam.

Thankfully, it had neither snowed nor rained in the
night. The water now filled the lake at an increasing rate,
and its rising was ever more noticeable, the empty buildings and spartan trees standing in its new shallows serving
further to accentuate this progress.

I arrived at the dam by ten. It was a cold day, but I sought
no shelter. Few of the people I encountered paid any
attention to me, and as far as I knew none of them was
aware of the visit or of my purpose there.

I enquired after Mary Latimer, but was told simply that she had neither yet been found nor seen elsewhere. Their pretence of searching for her had ceased.

By eleven there was still no sign of the delegation, and my presence for so long in one place was beginning to attract unwelcome attention.

Shortly afterwards, I left the dam and followed the road down the valley. It was from this direction they would come. I might meet them here away from anyone else and then usefully spend my time with them in explaining what they could expect to see. I had prepared several short speeches, and was convinced, after all my other preparations, that I had answers to all their questions.

I waited on the same rise from which I had a fortnight earlier watched the departing families. The long downhill curve of the road was visible ahead of me, and I saw far to the south where the green of the winter countryside gave way to the darker irregularities of the towns as they grew together.

By midday, still sitting alone on the cold rock, I gave voice to my curses, and as though in response to this, and just as I rose and gathered up my belongings, a carriage appeared at the bend in the road. Checking my appearance in the looking-glass I carried, I went down to await its arrival.

I raised my hand to the driver and he leaned back to confer with someone inside before coming on to me. The breath of the four horses clouded the air and a froth of phlegm covered their mouths.

The carriage door opened and a young man I had never before seen climbed down. He came to me and asked me who I was. I told him and he shouted this back to the carriage. A window was lowered and two other faces looked out. I recognized both men from my interview.

'Where were you?' one shouted. 'We imagined something terrible had happened to you.'

'I've been waiting,' I said, at a loss to understand him.

'You were expected in Halifax yesterday afternoon,' he said. 'We waited for you there.'

'Your letter said you were to come here.'

'Yes. After *first* having conferred with you in town. The fact is, our journey here today may not have been entirely necessary.'

'Or wanted,' the man beside him said.

There was laughter inside the carriage.

The younger man beside me bowed his head at hearing this, as though to disassociate himself from it, and perhaps to ease my own discomfort at hearing it.

'Your letter made no mention whatsoever of my coming to Halifax,' I called to the man in the carriage. It was difficult to conceal the anger in my voice.

The second man at the window took out a silver flask and drank from it.

'Is it far?' he called to me.

'Far?'

'To the dam, to the water, whatever it is we've come all this way to be impressed by.' He looked at the moor all around him. 'Is it always this cold?'

I said nothing in reply

'You'd better get in,' he said. 'We are six.'

'And a dozen lucky others left back at the hotel,' his companion said. More laughter erupted behind them.

The young man beside me said, 'None of us saw the actual letter that was sent.' His voice was low and conspiratorial. 'This was the Chairman's idea. I wonder if some of them can even begin to imagine the existence of the dam or the water or what is being achieved here.' He held out his hand to me. 'I'm Smith,' he said. 'From Durham. I came because they are about to embark on a similar project there.'

'And your part in it?'

I held out my own hand, and the moment he grasped it he said, 'Very much the same as yours here. Supervising overseer and consultant responsible for the evacuation, drainage and reclamation.' He took pride in the title, and I regretted that the contaminated baton of hopeful expectation had just that instant passed between us.

'So that's what I am,' I said.

He looked at me uncertainly for a moment and then smiled. He withdrew his hand and gestured towards the carriage.

Inside were others I recognized, and they greeted me as though we were great friends, as though I were one of them. The air was thick with smoke. Wicker baskets filled the luggage nets. I was offered a cigar, which I declined, and a drink which I accepted, though I was reluctant to take it. My face, hands and feet were numb from waiting.

I was quizzed again on why I hadn't gone to the hotel. I was told that all my expenses would have been met. One man told me he had visited the valley two years previously, before work on the dam had started. He looked out of the window as he spoke and said that the place looked just as miserable now as it had done then.

I saw that Smith remained uneasy in their company. I guessed him to be four or five years younger than myself, and I knew well enough why he was examining me. He looked at the dirt on my clothes, at my bags and satchel and the hold I kept on them.

We arrived finally at the dam. I was the first to climb down from the carriage. Our arrival brought the usual inquisitive crowd, smaller than formerly, but no less insistent on its right to be there.

The Board members were slow in alighting. Smith came to stand beside me. I greeted those who had gathered to watch and explained to them who these visitors were.

The others finally climbed down and put on their heavy coats. They all wore gloves, and I saw by their shoes that they would walk no distance, and certainly not over rough tracks or unmade roads. Most still had their cigars. They congregated briefly, held a whispered conversation, and then dispersed, some going to the dam and others coming to where I stood with the crowd.

I had expected the usual resentment and then hostility from the gathered men and women, but to my surprise – dismay, I might say – they stood entranced by – almost grateful for – the words of the man who now unexpectedly addressed them. He gave a small girl a silver coin, and when other children approached him with their hands out he gave them coins too, and they all ran among the adults showing off what they had been given.

Beside me, Smith whispered, 'Watch him. He's very good. He came to Durham last month.'

'They won't feel the same towards you once it starts happening,' I said.

'No, I know.'

But he knew then only what he had been told and what he wanted to believe.

I resented the crowd's acceptance of all the Board man said to them.

'Watch what happens at the first hostile response,' Smith said to me.

It came a few moments later. The man had been talking about the risks taken by the investors when a woman in the crowd called out to ask him what those risks were compared to the hardships currently being suffered by the people living there who were losing their homes.

Others took up the call. The Board man fell silent and hung his head. He stood like this until the shouting abated, and then he lifted his face and raised his hands. He began to tell them all that he understood perfectly their concerns and the upheavals through which they had lived this past year.

I stopped listening to him then, and looked beyond him to where the others had climbed the steps to the dam and had gathered to look out over the grave of the valley below. I knew how impressed they would be by all they saw there, the encircling view made even more dramatic by its distant frame of dazzling snow.

I was distracted from these thoughts by the sudden and enthusiastic burst of applause which rose all around me, and by Smith tugging at my sleeve and saying, 'See?'

I nodded, unaware of what had happened. I gathered from what was then said that some further compensation had been promised to those still remaining. To hear their applause you might think their lives had just been saved or made whole again.

'See?' Smith repeated.

'I see,' I told him.

The men high on the dam had by then spread

themselves along its entire length. They did not care how deep it sank into the water beneath them or how great was the weight pressing against every square foot of its surface.

Smith saw me looking. He understood my disappointment. He had not known what to expect of me, but he had expected more than he had found, and it was vital now, in his mind, for there to be a distance between us.

'They were talking on the way here of a naming ceremony,' he said.

'The Forge Valley Dam.'

'You sound convinced of that.'

'Then what?'

He indicated the man who had made the promises and handed out the silver coins.

'They're going to name it after him?'

'Nothing decided yet. But he's working for it. Someone will make the suggestion at the appropriate moment during their meeting next week and no one will be able to refuse him.'

I looked at the man, who in turn stood gazing up at the monument he had so cheaply secured for himself. Then he went to it and climbed each of the steps to its rim with a slow and measured stride, pausing every few paces to look around him at the revealed surroundings, and occasionally back down at us, growing ever smaller beneath him.

No one else approached the steps while he climbed, and when he reached the top those already standing there applauded him and he raised his hands to them. And then he turned slowly to look out over the lake, savouring the surprise and the spectacle of it before drawing his hands back to his face in delight and rejoicing at what he saw.

In all my time there it had never once occurred to me

that the lake and the dam would be named for anything other than the place they had drowned.

'See?' Smith said again, and he too went to climb the steps of the dam and to be part of the man's rejoicing.

48

Two days later the last of the hefted sheep were gathered in off the high land and penned prior to their sale and slaughter. They were the animals which could not be moved and there was no alternative to their killing. Fellmongers and butchers came from neighbouring towns to bid for them.

In total, over three hundred were brought down. Ten times that number had been gathered in the previous autumn, and these last few were poor specimens. Most of the locals came out to watch, and it was easy to imagine the profitable celebration the occasion might otherwise have been.

Most of the animals were bought by a monger with a contract to supply the militia and were slaughtered soon after being sold to him. I sought the man out and intro-duced myself. I asked him if any balance in the loss of value of the sheep was to be made up by the Board and he became suspicious of me and wanted to know what business it was of mine to ask. I left him and wandered among the pens.

The sorry-looking creatures were killed in a small enclosure bordering the chapel. The slaughtermen worked with hammers and knives, either crushing the animals' skulls or stunning them sufficiently with their blows to slit their throats before they were fully aware of what was happening to them.

The dirty fleeces were stripped from the sheep in a single piece, occasionally while they were still in their death throes and feebly struggling against something they could not possibly comprehend. Heads, tails and feet were chopped off and thrown into piles. Bellies were slit open and innards pulled out and left to slide over the ground at the slaughtermen's feet. The carcases were then further reduced, some quartered, some halved, and the meat was cast on to a wagon. I watched the process almost mesmerized, calculating that each living creature was reduced to these pieces in less than a minute.

It was bitterly cold, but the smell of the warm blood and viscera filled the air. Crows congregated along the chapel wall, the bravest of them alighting on the mess of innards while they were still fresh and steaming. The men busy at the killing did little to discourage the birds, threatening them only when they scavenged on the carts of piled meat.

I stood with an old man who guarded the chapel entrance. I remarked on the day's business with him. He was the same man who had long ago asked me about the wife and children I did not have.

'First the animals, then the trees, then the dead,' he said, meaning the arrangements already made for the coppices on the far side of the valley to be felled, and after that for the long-awaited removal of the bodies from the burial ground.

I asked him if any of the sheep being slaughtered were his own.

'Twenty or thirty,' he said, gesturing vaguely in the direction of the penned animals.

I asked him if he didn't find the whole business distressing. He looked at me without feeling and asked me how I imagined it usually happened. A group of children arrived beside us, each holding aloft a dirty tail.

The militia butcher came to us. He asked the old man what we were discussing, and I told him it was none of his business.

'I'm talking to him,' the butcher said. I saw that he and the old man were acquainted.

'He thinks there's a better way to kill a sheep,' the old man said, and the pair of them laughed.

'And what might that be?' the butcher said to me. He chewed on something and then spat heavily at my feet. I looked down. 'Mutton. I get a sense of the worthlessness of the stuff by chewing on it raw. Not that it matters in this case, not where this lot's going. Want some?' He took out another piece from his pocket and held it in my face. I turned away. Then he offered it to the old man, who pressed the meat into his mouth and sucked hard on it.

49

A further three days passed, during which time I spoke to no one.

I went again to Mary Latimer's home, but found it just as I had left it, another empty dwelling abandoned, if not to the water itself, then to the emptiness and desolation which preceded it and which now spread outwards in all directions from it.

I searched for her in my usual desultory fashion, calling for her, and still unsettled by the sound of my own un-answered voice coming back to me.

Elsewhere, rumour begat rumour, and the tales needed little encouragement to thrive and to persuade those who repeated them that she was alive and well and living else-where, that their concern and my insistence upon it had been unwarranted. Only the old woman remained genuinely concerned, but she too refused to indulge me and preferred to remain silent rather than to confirm my own dark thoughts.

All talk now was of the new promises made by the Board, and I sensed that those who remained felt a perverse sense of pride in what they believed their stubbornness had achieved for them.

The departure of the Board men had been as inauspicious and as disappointing as their arrival. I was summoned to join them prior to their going, but they showed little real interest in what I had to say to them.

After barely an hour of reassuring and congratulating themselves, they returned to their carriage. The baskets of food and drink were taken down and I was invited to share their meal. The blinds were drawn and we sat in a stale gloom as we ate.

Finally the time came for them to go, and I was again praised. My work here would not go unnoticed or un-rewarded, they said.

I left the carriage accompanied only by Smith, who walked with me to the water's edge. I asked him if the others wouldn't be anxious for him to return to them so they might leave, but he gave me an evasive answer and put me on my guard. He said he had hoped to see where I lived and I pointed through the falling darkness in the direction of my house.

'Did they tell you to come with me?' I said.

He looked away from me. 'They wanted me to talk to you about the rest of your time here.' He coughed to clear his throat.

'Three more months. By which time their glorious duckpond will be filled to overflowing.'

'They wanted me to let you know how surprised they were to see the water already so high in advance of the spring thaw. They didn't expect to see half so much.'

I began then to understand what he was having such difficulty telling me.

'Do they believe my work here to be finished?'

'There is no question of you not receiving your agreed salary.'

'Do they want me to leave?'

'There are new schemes already being prepared and undertaken elsewhere. My own in Durham. Others in Derbyshire. Over the hills there in Lancashire and Westmorland. Or, if you'd prefer, further south, the Home Counties. I believe there is even a new scheme in Shropshire.' He stopped abruptly, conscious of having said too much.

'Am I to understand that I'm being offered another contract to undertake work elsewhere?'

'I don't ... they believe that your abilities and talents ...'

'What? That they are now being wasted here?'

'That they ... that you ...'

That I now formed an unnecessary link between what was happening here and them, and that they finally wanted that connection severed.

'Save your breath,' I told him.

'I'm in no position to argue with them,' he said.

'You never will be. Never.'

He acknowledged this with a sigh.

'And presumably their promises of further compensation are lies,' I said.

He was about to answer when someone called to him from the carriage.

'Did they suggest a date to you?' I asked him.

'Nothing specific.'

'But the sooner the better?'

He looked around him. 'They can't imagine anyone choosing to spend a whole winter up here.'

The voice called again.

'You'd better get back to them,' I told him.

'What shall I tell them?'

'Tell them you told me everything they told you to tell me.'

'It was why they wanted you to come to the hotel. So we might have had this conversation there.'

'And so that I might see everything I've been deprived of these past months.'

He held out his hand to me. 'There's a civic reception next week – it's more than an annual meeting – at which the success of the scheme will be announced and celebrated.'

'Are you invited?' I asked him.

'They want to parade me in front of prospective investors. These men never stand still.' He began to walk away from me.

'Tell them I'll consider their proposals,' I called after him.

I saw then, watching him go, that just as my departure might sever the connection between those men and this place, so, equally, my remaining here would destroy completely whatever small chance I might still have had of being further employed by them, to dance again on the end of their strings. The future beyond this valley had counted for little in my reckoning of late; it was now a forbidden country to me.

Smith disappeared into the darkness and then became visible again briefly as he approached the light of the carriage lantern. He paused and raised his hand to me and I waved back. There was some further small commotion as he climbed aboard and was beset by questions.

As I walked home it started to snow again, lightly at first, the flakes falling widely separated in the windless night, but then ever thickening and flowing in currents as I reached the middle valley.

50

And with the killing of the animals, so it seemed that a long-delayed rush of events was set in motion in the place. For after the slaughtermen came the woodcutters, and after these came the men to dig up the graves. The sickening body which had for so long lain barely moving on its deathbed had now begun to writhe and to convulse and to fill the air with its moans.

This was what I saw then, in those few unstoppable days, and it was what I afterwards remained to bear witness to.

The woodcutters came, but kept themselves apart. They worked mostly downriver and on the far side of the valley. They cut at a rapid pace, as though the contraction of time above the dam now also pertained below it, and they burned in giant fires that wood which they did not take away with them.

As might be imagined, this sudden loss of even the leafless trees created a dramatic change in the appearance of the valley. The men were under instruction to clear the slopes completely, to leave nothing which might obstruct the flow of water should the sluices need to be fully opened in an emergency.

The smoke from their fires thickened and gathered in a pall, kept low by the winds which played constantly above it, and watching this interplay of warm and cold air, the smoke looked almost as though it were liquid flowing uphill and harried into turbulence as it rose. And in the falling dusk it even seemed as though the land itself were melting and being drawn away. The smell of burning was in everything and the ground stayed blackened and pocked.

Carts came and went for three days and the hillside was cleared. Some of the local men wandered among the hewn stumps and smouldering ground, looking like the survivors of a great disaster. I watched them from a distance, high on the dam, but did not join them.

More snow fell, this time lying lower down the hillsides. Further up the valley, the paths were blocked and the winter-born streams frozen over. Opposite my house, a small waterfall – previously no more than a glissade of spray from one scarp ledge to another – froze overnight into a brilliantly white ribbon, seemingly more substantial and permanent in this state than when it had been alive and flowing. I had noticed it only recently, and now the frozen course stood like a giant thermometer, a constant reminder of the cold that was settling down through the land as insidiously and relentlessly as the water was driving up through it from below; air, water and earth all now fixed together in their various combinations, freezing and thawing, transforming and remaking until soon everything would be unalterably changed.

It occurred to me to wonder what might happen if all the feeder streams froze, or if the rising water encountered frozen and impenetrable strata. A month ago the prospect of investigating such a possibility might have intrigued or even excited me. But not now. Now it was merely one more pointless conundrum within a tangle of pointless conundrums. A month ago my charts and instruments would all have been made ready; now my reckonings were passing thoughts of no more consequence than the countless other trivialities which filled my days.

The staff of my authority had been taken from me and I felt its loss keenly in everything I did.

Usually, the snow started to fall in the late afternoon and continued through to midnight, when it abated for several hours before resuming two or three hours before dawn, afterwards falling until mid or late morning.

I saw the land as it might once have been beneath its mantle of ice. I searched the shallows of the lake and in places saw the mash of crystals gathering in the slower currents. I saw a white line form across the wall of the dam where the foam of the waves hit the cold stone and froze there in its shadow.

51

On the fifth day of my snow-bound isolation, following an afternoon and night during which there were no fresh falls, I made my way laboriously down to the mine road. This was the day when the men were due to come and dig up the graves. A final line drawn through my list of obligations.

It was a clear day, a winter's day a man might otherwise delight in, and for the first time in a month I could not see a single cloud in the sky, only a slight darkening from the washed-out blue to the palest grey of the western horizon.

The mine road was clear for much of its length. Some freak of the valley's configuration meant that the winds which came at it from the west drove the snow uphill into drifts, leaving the narrow bottom with only a thin covering.

I met a boy who confirmed that the grave-diggers (if such they could still be called) had arrived.

I encountered the men around a fire by the chapel door. I recognized some of the wreckers who had come a month earlier, but Tozer was not among them, and I learned from the man who had taken his place that he had been fired by the Board following the previous visit.

As we spoke, a heavy cart appeared and came slowly along the path leading to the chapel.

A few of the locals came with it, and with them came a preacher I had not before seen. He wore a wide-brimmed hat, with a sash of the brightest scarlet draped over his shoulders. He walked past me without speaking and climbed on to the chapel wall, and there he began a sermon, telling the diggers to wait until he was finished. He made them all uneasy with his words, condemning them for what they were about to do. The locals applauded each of his short, calculated phrases. The man's hot breath formed in plumes around his head, and steam rose from his chest and shoulders to wreathe him further in his overblown piety.

A woman came to stand beside me. 'You trespass against us, you surely do,' she said to me, her words little more than a cold hiss. Those standing around us nodded in agreement with her.

In the burial ground the diggers gathered more closely together.

'We will not leave the dead if they are not to be allowed to rest in peace,' the preacher shouted.

The devil in me wanted to call out and ask him

what he expected the dead to do – did he think they might all rise from their coffins and swim to the surface of the coming water like so many silvery fishes?

When his sermon was finished the man dropped his head and clasped his hands in vigorous prayer. I did not hear his exact words for the murmuring of the men and women all around me, and because of the rising claver of the gulls arrived to stake their own noisy claim in the empty future of the place. It occurred to no one to ask whence the birds came, so far from any sea – as in most other things, there is no wonder here, no awe.

The grave-diggers dug quickly, piling the snow into mounds before attacking the hard earth beneath. The few remaining headstones were lifted and carried to the side of the chapel and stacked there.

The first of the rotten coffins soon appeared, but little was done to identify the occupants of the raised boxes. It had been the custom here to open old ground and to bury family members on top of each other. Consequently, the more recent burials rested only a few feet below the surface, and the diggers were surprised and pleased to encounter these so easily.

In some instances the wood of the coffins remained sufficiently intact for them to be lifted whole, but mostly the boxes had succumbed and collapsed, and they and the remains they held were shovelled into sacks before being taken to the waiting cart.

The same woman came back to me as the others dispersed. She said how pleased I must be feeling with myself after all I had achieved there. Again, I made no reply to her. She said that Almighty God, though forgiving, would never forgive me for what I had brought into being on that day. Had I chosen to speak, I might have agreed with her.

The preacher left his perch on the wall and came to me. He stood beside me for several minutes watching the labouring men. Then he looked out over the lake and traced its outline, dark now against the whiteness of the land. He was clearly impressed by what he saw. I braced myself against the first of his own damning remarks, but instead he held out his hand to me and introduced himself.

'You are not a well-liked man,' he said, his tone tempered by amusement. 'They wanted me to say more on the matter.' He nodded to those passing us by. 'I came overnight. Interminable hours spent in prayer. I don't know what they expected of me, but I don't doubt that I too have disappointed them. They told me the multitude of ways I might condemn you. I wonder that you are not already in flames.' He paused. 'A short prayer was said for the woman who lost her sister to the asylum. Your name was mentioned in connection with her.'

'How soon will they take the bodies?' I asked him, refusing to be drawn.

He looked again over the lake. 'Would it surprise you or dismay you to learn that I am a shareholder in the scheme? This and others like it.'

'My stocks of surprise and dismay are both long since exhausted where the Board and its works are concerned,' I said.

'I understand your feelings. Perhaps I should have come here before. An acquaintance of mine said he had encountered you in the autumn.'

'The historian?'

'He said even then that you would succeed in your work and that the world here would be changed for ever.'

'And is he, too, a shareholder?'

'Of course. These things are wise investments. Men of our limited means must risk what we can. Surely you your-self have some financial commitment in the work.'

I told him it seemed scarcely any risk and he smiled at this and fluttered his hand.

'I attend all the shareholders' meetings,' he said.

'And you find no conflict between your profits and the work going on here today?'

'Why should I? There are plenty of others always ready to stand in the way of progress.'

I turned away from him to watch the diggers. Another fire had been lit, but this one burned with more smoke than flame, fed as it was with the rotten wood and earth of the coffins. I saw where grey bones spilled from the sacks on the cart.

'Will you bless the remains?' I asked him.

'It's what they want. They want me to stay the night, but the word is for more snow.'

'Do you live far away?'

'Far enough. You could leave with me if you were prepared.'

I shook my head at the empty offer.

The wagon with its load of boxes was brought closer to the chapel.

'It was never a much-used place,' he said. 'Whatever they might have told you. A few blue ribbon bands on holidays, visiting fanatics, healers. Did you imagine it to have once been the spiritual centre of the place? No. They are affectionate for it now only because it is the last of what they have to lose. Had I stayed tonight, my prayers would have been short. Like you, I do what is expected of me and no more. I fit into the expectations of others more than I fulfil my own intentions. It is a commoner path than you might imagine.' He again held out his hand to me, then put on his gloves and left me.

I was alone in the company of the diggers. There was now little method in their work and they left behind them as much as they retrieved.

Beneath us, the gulls settled on the water and drifted there in motionless silence.

The glow from the fires, and the lanterns and the black shapes of the men moving among them, remained visible to me as I made my way home, and all around the lying snow cast its strange and shifting patterns of metallic glare and shadow in the falling dusk. I need hardly say it, but if ever a vision of Hell existed in the mind of a simple, fearful man, then this was surely it.

52

There have been times these past days, especially when my eye is caught by something I wrote or mapped during my early weeks here, when I cannot do other than wonder at how much I have lost. I do not say this loss is akin to a loss of faith – for that would be to glorify something far removed from the glorious – but it is as though I have been a sleepwalker, a man who sees the distant cliff edge, the ever-steepening or crumbling slope, and yet who insists on marching boldly forward, knowing full well that after a thousand such bold steps, a single one will take him over the edge and into oblivion.

I am a man between elements, just as this place is, a man who has long since ceased to hug the shore and who has cast himself out into deeper waters to navigate the shoals and reefs of uncertainty and deception there, to make new landfall and forever afterwards to wander the wrack between all that lies behind him and all that lies ahead.

I know these are over-elaborate and convoluted thoughts, but such, increasingly, is the natural cast of my mind.

There is a stronger draught than usual this evening, and the room will not allow a single good candle to burn without it constantly spitting and guttering, and the result of this – this crop of flattened pearls – lies scattered on my table like windfall fruit around its tree.

Is there a valid distinction to be drawn, I wonder, between a man despising himself for what he is, what he has allowed himself to become, and another man despising himself for the excuses he makes?

These winds and the cold seeping into my bones are once again death to all clear and rational thought.

53

Mary Latimer's floating corpse was eventually sighted two days later by a man crossing the dam who saw it thirty feet below him on the rising level, face down and close to the wall, and moving slowly back and forth in the sluggish current there.

I was not sent for; a miner I encountered told me what had happened.

Everyone else was already gathered on the dam or on the shore, and had a single one of them possessed a boat or even a skiff, then the retrieval of the body might have been effected in minutes. Some fell silent at my approach, but others, by far the greater number, did nothing to hide their feelings from me.

'What need would we ever have of boats?' said the man I asked.

At that distance the body was not clearly revealed, merely an uncertain shape in the water. There were no women, only men, on the rim of the dam looking down. The few children on the shore were held at a distance by their mothers.

The men on the dam had ropes, and one, I saw, had made a harness for himself, and his companions were in the process of lowering him as I arrived. I saw how futile the attempt would be. Below them, the body continued to wash back and forth against the dam wall. The man descended only half-way to the water before calling to be pulled back up. He stood breathless, tugging at the ropes which cut into his shoulders, his only real achievement having been to verify that the body was that of Mary Latimer.

As I approached closer this same man repeated everything to me. I was still their official seal, still their blotter rolled in sanction over every fresh event. He stood waiting for my praise, but I said nothing, and went past him to where the others stood rewinding their ropes.

I looked over the rim of the dam at the corpse below.

And where will you go? It is something I prefer not to think about until Martha has gone and I have convinced myself there was nothing I could have done to prevent her going. Have arrangements already been made? Arrangements are always made, you of all people should know that.

She was still face down. Her legs were spread and only one arm showed. Her head rested closest to the dam and she was sucked gently back and forth by the natural pull of the structure on the water.

The voices faded around me, and I wondered how many of them had expected or hoped to see my own corpse down there, for I saw only too clearly how much more fitting an ending that would have been in their scheme of things.

The men still holding the ropes stood undecided about what to do next. One of them held an iron hook, and he suggested grappling for the body, snagging it and then pulling it to the shore. Another suggested returning to the shore and throwing the hook from there, but I saw how unlikely this was to succeed. The body lay at least fifty yards from the shallows, and the hook and rope were heavy.

Eventually, the man holding the hook looked to me for advice, and I recommended the first plan. Others nodded in agreement with this, and in the midst of this concurrence the man came to me and handed me the hook.

'You do it,' he said, making it clear to me that I still had some unavoidable involvement in the matter. It was a small trap and I had entered it.

I took the rope and went back to the edge. The body below had not moved.

My first instinct was to throw the hook into the water further out, let it sink and then draw it towards me until it caught on the corpse, but I saw what damage this might do, and so instead I lowered it down the slope of the dam, letting it slide over the blocks until it swung only a few feet above the body. A woman on the shore started wailing and her voice was echoed by others; several of the children began to cry.

I expected further advice on how best to secure the body, but the men beside me remained silent and watchful.

I unwound several more coils until the hook disappeared beneath the surface of the water. I calculated how many days had passed since Mary Latimer had gone missing. It was at least fifteen, possibly closer to twenty. I tried to imagine what that length of submersion would do to flesh and bone, and I was grateful, looking down, that she remained partially clothed.

My first attempt to secure her was a failure. I let the hook sink alongside her until the rope rested against her shoulder, but then I lifted it too quickly and it came up out of the water without catching her.

As I made my second attempt, it resumed snowing, a fine, sifting snow which covered us all in its powder and melted into the lake below.

This time I let the hook draw beneath Mary Latimer's outstretched arm, and feeling the drag of the rope against her, I pulled more sharply upwards. I had expected some resistance, and then for the rope to remain taut, but again I had been over-optimistic, and instead of catching in the corpse, the hook came through it, perhaps tearing it in the chest or beneath the arm, before rising out of the water with a piece of cloth attached. The rope felt loose for an instant, and then the hook fell back, striking Mary Latimer on her head and causing the whole of her upper body to sink beneath the surface. There were further cries from the shore, and this time from the men beside me.

I pulled the hook back out of the water and waited for the waves to subside and for the corpse to become still. I thought for a moment, watching it hang suspended beneath the surface, that it might not come back up at all, that my clumsy exertions might have been enough to send it back to the depths and for it to remain there.

But eventually it settled on the surface and the ripples around it died. I let more of the rope sink beneath it, and then moved several paces to one side, so that on this occasion when I struck I would be striking into her chest, her ribs, where the hook might lodge more firmly. These were all silent calculations, and I believe every man beside me made them.

This time the rope rose beside her neck and the hook found some purchase beneath her, and feeling it connect, I gave several shorter tugs, forcing it deeper into whatever it held. Thus caught, Mary Latimer spun and rolled, and for the first time she was turned face up to us, her head a foot beneath the water, but thankfully the surface was so broken by her motions that none of us, neither I nor the watching men beside me, could see her clearly.

The man closest to me told me to start pulling. Others began walking back across the dam. The shore would need to be cleared. I, too, began to walk, knowing that with every step I took the hook might yet come loose and everything would have to be attempted again. I knew myself incapable of doing any more than I had already done.

I moved slowly, testing the grip, and watching as the body below began to float along the dam wall.

It turned as it came. Her arm rose above the surface, her limp hand held in the semblance of a wave. The rope then wrapped itself around her neck, further securing her. Her legs rose and fell as they were dragged behind her, looking from above as though she were moving them of her own accord.

It took several minutes to drag her the length of the dam. I descended to the new shore. The women and children were held back. The snow began to fall more heavily, cutting out the wider view.

Two men waded into the shallows to retrieve the body. They had once been shepherds and each man held a crook. I stopped pulling and the corpse continued to the shore under its own momentum. I let the rope fall into the sludge at my feet.

I stood alone, but rather than go to join those gathering in the shallows, I climbed back up the steps of the dam to stand above them.

The upper and the lower valley were now hidden by the falling snow, and nothing of the wider surroundings or of the sky above was visible. All I could see was the small, lost world beneath me. I tried to look beyond this, but saw only as far as its white, shrouded edges where the gulls still hovered disturbed and ghostlike above the water, fading and then magically reappearing as they came and went through the falling snow.

The men on the shore finally reached the body. The other watchers came closer. All Mary Latimer's remaining clothes had been stripped from her by the water. The crying women and children were no longer held back.

I turned from the distant, closing view back to the silent drama beneath me. I saw the outspread corpse at its centre. I saw too the frayed rope still tied to one of Mary Latimer's ankles, her face and her nakedness now covered in decency by a dark cloth, beneath which the water streamed from her and lay around her in a pool, making her an island amid the wet.

54 _____

Five more days have passed, and it has snowed with increasing vigour during that time. It falls even when the sky looks ready to grow clear, but then darkens again with the trigger of the sun. Sometimes there is a wind and the powder is driven into the smallest spaces and piled in mounds higher than a standing man. At other times it falls in a stillness of large flakes which hang in the air as though reluctant to settle and forsake the intricacies of their individual designs.

As long predicted, I am trapped in my house here. Beneath me, the pattern of walls and enclosures along the valley sides is lost in the all-encompassing whiteness; peaks are rounded and depressions filled, and a whole new aspect is created. A man might guess at the lost paths, but he can no longer align himself to familiar landmarks and know his way for sure.

Only the unfrozen lake shows dark through the white, stretching now in every direction as though it had been there since Creation.

Christmas and the New Year have come and gone in the weather, and I am reminded of the tales of Arctic explorers wintering in their vessels caught in the ice, locked solid, slowly crushed and starved, and yet still celebrating these holidays, still putting on their pantomimes and lantern shows.

I see again and again how I have been used here as the world around me has been altered and shaped to the profit and loss of water.

My barometer – that grinning Jeremiah of an instrument – mocks me from its place on the wall and has shown not the slightest sign of movement for these past five days.

I search the night sky in vain for the waning moon and familiar constellations. But just as here below, so too are my celestial guides denied to me.

55 _____

In my dream of those nights all is different, of course. In my dream, Mary Latimer's corpse, instead of being dragged to the shore, rises against the dam and comes up effortlessly out of the water on the end of my rope, and I look down at her, mesmerized by her slow spinning and by the way her arms move back and forth with the motion as though she were performing some dreaming dance of the dead. And in my dream I again become anxious that the hook will come loose and that she will fall and this time sink for ever into the depths and never afterwards be retrieved. Ice has already sealed shut the place from which she has risen and the falling snow is turning the surface beneath her white.

She absorbs the twisting motion of the rope as she rises, her head tipping back and falling loosely from side to side, as though she were searching the rim above her for the face of her rescuer. The spinning motion of her arms gradually slows and stops, and then they begin to flap gently, rising and falling from her sides as though she were a swimmer not yet come to the surface, but calm, and sure of her arrival there.

I can see down on to her unclothed breasts. Her legs remain firmly together, joined along their length to her toes, and the water which runs from them falls in a single stream and is feathered to spray beneath her, and she seems almost to rise on this spray, as though the trickling water were the trail of powder behind a rocket or a flare. Her hair, at first plastered close to her face by the water, quickly dries and resumes its more natural shape, falling back from her eyes and her mouth.

I see all of this looking down at her. I see nothing of the corruption and decay of her time in the water. I see nothing of the river worms and leeches which cling to her flesh in places. I see nothing of the rope still fastened to her ankles.

She comes up to me at an even, steady pace, and seems an interminable time in coming. So long, in fact, that I have ample time to look around me and to study those on the shore below to see if they too see what I see. They are mostly silent now, but with the occasional uncontainable cry rising above them, and it occurs to me to communicate with them and to ask them for their assistance. But other than look down at them, and they up at me, nothing passes between us.

Further out, I see the passage of the shadows of clouds on the water, as though giant fish were already swimming close beneath its surface.

And as she comes higher, so the snow briefly ceases

falling and the winter sun rushes in to fill the valley with its bright and searching light, illuminating us all in this drama of impossible resurrection. I see the molten disc itself distort and then re-form on the frozen surface, and I shift my position so that it lies directly beneath her, so that what little water still falls from her falls directly on to the pale orb and fractures it further, and so that, in my dream, in my unknowing imagination at least, I might believe it to be some underwater pedestal upon which she has for so long awaited her rescue, and in whose blinding, healing glow she now rises towards me.

And so where all of this is most real to me, where my heart beats its wildest in anticipation of what is to happen next, I stand and watch as the drowned woman comes level with the top of the dam, as she rises above it and looks directly at me, as she raises her arm to point to me, and then as she slowly opens her mouth to call out to me that she is saved and that I am her saviour, but where instead of the words there comes only more of the same dark water pouring like bile from her lips.

I wake then, in the dead of the night, my bedclothes in disarray on the floor beside me, and as the kaleidoscopic fragments of dream, memory and reality slowly reassemble themselves into a shape more closely resembling what has truly happened, I find myself gasping for air, as though I and not she had just then struggled to the surface, lungs fit to burst, filmed with sweat and not water where I burned, and unable to control to even the slightest degree the violent tremor of my shaking chest and limbs.

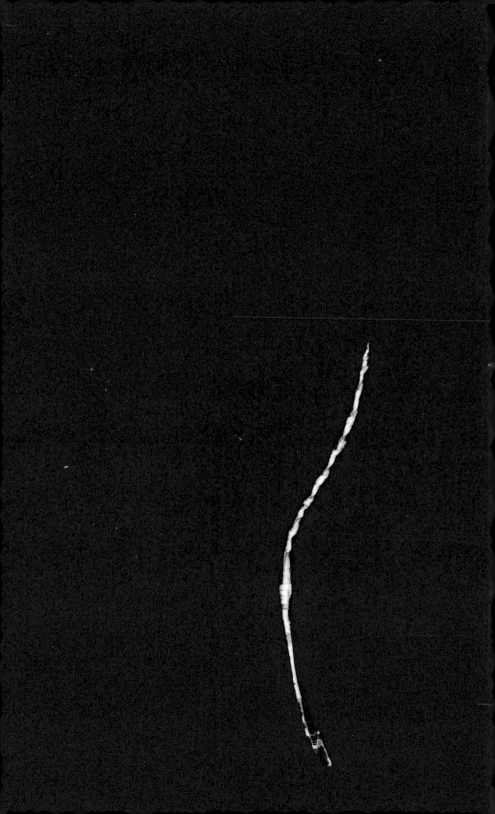